CrashBoomLove

Withdrawn

A Novel in Verse

Juan Felipe Herrera

University of New Mexico Press   *Albuquerque*

crash
boom
love

14 13 12 11 10   9 10 11 12 13

ISBN-13: 978-0-8263-2114-5

Library of Congress Cataloging-in-Publication Data

Herrera, Juan Felipe.
   CrashBoomLove : a novel in verse / Juan Felipe Herrera. —1st ed.
   p. cm
   SUMMARY : After his father leaves home, sixteen-year-old César Garcia lives
with his mother and struggles through the painful experiences of growing up
as a Mexican American high school student.
   ISBN 0-8263-2114-3 (paper: alk. paper)
   1. Mexican Americans—Juvenile fiction. [1. Mexican Americans—Fiction.
2. High schools—Fiction. 3. Schools—Fiction.] I. Title.
   PZ7.H432135 Cr 1999
   [Fic]—dc21

                           99-6603
                             CIP

A Mary Burritt Christiansen Poetry Series book.

The Mary Burritt Christiansen Endowed Memorial Poetry Series is intended as
a mechanism for the publication of significant works of poetry from an
international body of contributors.

contents

THE MIRROR

Por el canto se conoce al pájaro.
A bird is known by its song.

BROKEN FINGERNAILS

El perro manda al gato, y el gato a su cola.
The dog bosses the cat, and the cat its tail.

HANGING IN SPACE

El pez por su boca muere.
A fish dies by its mouth.

YELLOW ROOM

Todo cambia.
Everything changes.

A CAPELLA

El agua es blanda, la piedra dura,
pero, gota a gota, hace cavadura.
Water is soft, rocks are hard,
but, drop by drop, water finds a way.

Gracias to De Wolf High School in Fresno, Ms. Maureen Sharkey's class most of all, for critical notes and jousts, to the AVID students at Laton High for their stories, Robert Segura, my step-son, for sharing his difficult moments and experiences, my children: Almusol, Joaquín, Joshua and Marlene who carved their own individual pathways through school, Margarita Luna Robles, for giving me the inside notes. Gracias to Andrea Otañez, for her faith in this novel and her editorial insights. Aprecio to Lauro Flores for his Spanish grammar edits and friendship. A high-five to Dominic Ricardo who checked my style. To Mr. Gary Giannoni. To Heather Henson for giving me the initial writing sparks.

I bow to all my teachers for their guidance throughout my elementary, middle and high school years, all of them, the ones who looked into my eyes and walked me to the songs—thank you Ms. Sampson, Mr. Hayden, Mr. Wightman, Mr. Harrison Maxwell, Mr. Shuster, Mr. Petrich and Ms. Steiger, who stood behind me and my artwork when the going got tough. To all the students of the San Joaquin Valley, all valleys and all territories of the world slipping and crashing into unprecedented changes.

To my mother, Lucha, who was my first teacher, who taught me from magazines, newspaper cutouts, and old books she found in Good Will stores, to my father who spoke with tender words.

For Estovan Ramirez and André Tijerina who made it through high school. For Desi Lugo, who's on her way. For Li'l Ray, in spirit, always.

To my nephews and nieces, grandchildren Jeremiah and Rainsong; to all students, their caring schools, writing their stories, being and speaking who they are—around the world.

the mirror

Por el canto se conoce al pájaro
A bird is known by its song

last photograph with my father

Don't know how it all started. The frozen feeling,
this fender inside wanting to crash against everything.
Blown out blue night. My face.

That's me.
See the kid with a buzzed head.

Kinky overalls, bluish and acrylic spray
fat letters down the pants. Fists curled
like bike locks. Mama says, Don't be so angry.

Just making it up. I say.
Just making it up. In the kitchen with Selena on,
her hard black guitar eyes.

My eyes hard too. Like my father César's.
He's gone. With his new family in Denver.
Toña, Benita, his other kids.
Other wife, Olivia.
Mama says *paciencia*[1] like she says go to your room.
I was born on the road. That's all I know.

1. patience

Road of black starry grapes
waiting to crash,
that burn on wire vines.

Grapes pruned and pulled.
Grapes thrown cut and dropped dry.

They dry in the fiery red dust of Fowlerville.
Fowlerville, say it out loud. Say it biting my lips.

Father carries me in his arms. A torn brown
photograph I keep on the wall.

Campesino[2] shirt blue,
our trailer in tin.

Don't lose this *foto*,
she tells me. Mama Lucy.
Back at the kitchen window. Apartment # 9—
"C" Street, Westside barrio. Stare with my hard eyes.
Out into the night. Disappear.

2. farm worker

mama lucy's
address book

Lucy sings
to Selena as she presses my white T.
White T. Black baggies. Weave belt.

School costume. My colors—Black,
Red. Black & Red. My face gets tight.
No blue, no sky things. No *chavala*[3] stuff.

Lucy writes sideways. On the kitchen table.
Into her tiny address book without addresses.

Writes about food.
About me, she tells me.

Today we received $170.00 from the Welfare.
One bag of oranges. One bag of bleached flour.
Two gallons of milk. Wheat bread. The doctor says
wheat bread is good for you.

Lucy writes proverbs too:
Dime con quien andas y te dire quien eres.
Tell me with whom you walk and
I will tell you who you are.

4   3. girl, sissy

Poetry stuff:
Juventud, divino tesoro.
Youth, divine treasure.

Snap off the stocking from my head.
Comb my hair. Gel it back into a torch.

Only went to third grade.
Remember, César? Mama Lucy says.

Granma pulled me out. Caught stealing clothes
with one of my friends. You, you are smart, César.
Be careful. Tenth grade, César.

Lucy sings off-key but I don't tell her.
Spelling queen, that was me, César. Things change.

We were so poor. Who else
would take care of my mother?
She says wetting the tip
of the yellow pencil with her tongue.

Things change—*Todo cambia.*
She tells me. I clench my teeth,
look at the lead on her lips.

Lucy kisses me. I wipe it off.
Lead & lipstick. Black and red.
My mother's colors.

Adiós, César, don't forget
your lunch. I grab it. Hide,

the brown bag under my jacket
when Sammy Luna arrives. Struts.

My *carnal*[4] Sammy
who knows the streets.

canadá in english

Mrs. Tinko says Canada.
She says Ontario. *Canadá*—I whisper in Spanish.
Canadá—to myself in the back row.

Next to Sammy
who inks a skull into his hand. Between
his thumb and his finger. I squint
at the chalkboard English. A greenish sea.

A tidal wave that floods me
with strange curled words. Can't read.

I say *Canadá*. My mouth opens as if
to bite a stolen apple. Then my face hardens again.

6   4. buddy, home boy

I want to raise my hand. My arm is an iron plank.
Fingers are rivets. My blood is electric.

I whisper *Canadá.*
Only to myself. In Spanish.
When no one is watching.

When no one is listening. I write *Canadá*
on the inside of my hand. Look up
to the tidal wave, you gotta look up, César,
I talk to myself like Mama Lucy.

Is Denver by *Canadá?*
When I left México as a kid, alone, Papi used to say,
I jumped off the train in El Norte, in Denver.
Learned English in the snow. Then he'd laugh.

"A penny for each word." He said.
"That's how I learned."

How do you say lápiz in English?
Pencil. Ah, pencil.
How do you say leche in English?
Milk, Ah, milk.
How about cielo?
Sky. Ah, sky.

Three words for
three pennies.

I look at the watery map
by the limp flag. Wonder
about my father. His other family. Look
without words in English. Squint without
words in Spanish.

Sammy elbows me and laughs
at my right hand. *Canadá* is for sissies, César.
Skulls—are for us.

can opener at the bottom of the sea

At *lonche*,[5]
I sit with Sammy who winks at Margarita.
And Miguel Tzotzil who always follows me.
Sammy is tall.
Face pocked, tiny blue bullets
on his neck and forehead, acne. Talks fast
as if someone is always breathing
down his neck, as if his own shadow
is an unpredictable serpent.

Miguel says he's from Chiapas, México.
Chiapas—sounds like *chavas*,
which means girls.

5. lunch

I don't eat cuz Lucy's food
is funny. Giant flour tortillas with red folded
tips at the ends.

Chorizo sausage stains.
Or potato tacos fried, hard like clams.

What are those? Sammy asks.
Taco clams? Corn clappers?
Sammy kicks my lunch bag
into the bushes. Laughs.

Mexican food is an oily ghost cloud
that follows me. Wherever I go.

I don't eat. Sammy throws
his bag of chips at my face.
Miguel takes out a can of pineapple juice,
tamales. A can opener.

Miguel Tzotzil is proud of his can opener.
He cleans it on his pants. It is tied to a yo-yo string
on his belt, clipped to his house keys.

My uncle Manuel works late at the laundry.
His fingers so crooked like *tornillos.*[6]
I live with him. He tells us in his singing Spanish.

6. screws

And your father, I ask?

He's in Chiapas, in Tuxtla Gutiérrez, *la capital,*[7]
with my brother, Mariano, and two sisters, Pascuala
and Marúch.

Do you have brothers and sisters?
He asks me.

Nod nah——
as I rub the sharp edge of my elbow
with my left hand.

A can opener?
He says smiling.

I want to go to sleep. Ride the ocean
magic. Fall deep into the dark jade leaves.
Roll down fast.

Rumble darkly. Sparkle
like a steel wheel that no one can see,
that runs free.

7. the capital

the bays of fundy

Lonche is over. Kids stream back
to class and sit in quiet rows.
The math building looms ahead of us,
a strange church. The football field
blurs in the horizon.

Under the stairs next to class.
Sitting on a window ledge
by Sammy. Carlos Johnson whistles in a wild
basketball shirt. Maxy Ortega, a short dude
in black, hunched.

Carlos Johnson and Maxy
check us out, make bets. See
who cries first from Charlie Horses.

We're outside in the back of school. Behind
the new Science trailers.
That's only three punches, Sammy! Hit him
harder, cries Maxy.

He's older, but
I hit Sammy's leg anyway. Carlos Johnson
calls him a *chavala,* so he digs his knuckles
into my leg with a flying fist.

New at Rambling West High.
Some kids I've seen
en los files.[8] Like Miguel.
Back from the labor camps.
My first week.

Just moved to Fowlerville. Father said—
no hay otra[9]—we had to do it.

Lucy did what he said. Like always.
Prays to a tiny altar she keeps by the bed.
Lights candles and counts the dark blood
colored beads on her rosary.

Now, Papi is gone.
Left alone again. New names.

New streets. More visits downtown
to the Welfare office. My face
gets harder.

My legs tighten into cables.
Screws everywhere. Bolts. Cold
blood pumps the rough sockets.

8. in the fields, labor camps
9. there's no other way

Sammy launches another fist. Think
of Mrs. Tinko talk about British Columbia.
Follow her red finger east across Canada
to the Bay of Fundy, in Nova Scotia.

Mrs. Tinko says the tidal waves
are sixty feet high. Hear the echoes.
Boil with the waves. Thunder.

Slam!
Slam! Another fist bolt.

Carlos and Maxy giggle
like *chavalas*. A tear rips
through the steel in my eyes.

white boy shoes

Xeng sits next to me and Miguel Tzotzil. Lunch.
Show him my shoes. New Air Tigers Lucy bought me.
Hide my tortillas in the wrinkled bag.

Miguel Tzotzil. Round face, deer eyes.
Says he likes his art class.

Today I mixed things, he says.
Made a sculpture of a boy
in flames. Paper. Glue and starch.
Brown, black-green. And runny pink.

13

He has two sides. One
dark with starry animal eyes.
Sun storm eyes. Saturn-ring lips.

The second head is silvery.
Super wire brain. Car face. Chrome teeth.
Green grill tears. Miguel stutters
arching his eyebrows.

Xeng laughs at us talking
in Spanish. He calls me out: "White boy shoes!"
Crunches them with his thick black steel toes.
Laughs out in a high squirrel voice—
white boy shoooooes!

Sammy and Maxy, slumped,
hands in front pockets,
a few feet away. Stand high. Stare deep.
White mama shoes! Xeng growls,
spits to one side.

Look at you! My face
in a rumble of waves.
Project boy shoes! I say.

Thunder. Tidal waves.
Sockets and rivets smash
against the fence. Bolts
and steely thread scrape
14   the asphalt ditch.

Blood and electricity
smear on the bench.
Lettuce confetti.

Sammy grins and makes
dog noises at Carlos.

Mr. Santos, vice principal,
squeezes my left arm. Jerks me and Xeng
to the office. My eyes roll back to Miguel Tzotzil
as he shrinks into a sad cloth ball on the bench.

Me and Xeng.
Alone with our nervous feet. A Mexican and a Hmong.
In the office. Rubber shoes keep us apart
and together.

mama lucy's story

I visit the nuns
at St. Anns. Lucy

says it's an emergency.
Maybe, you'll change your ways, she says,
blowing the long gray-black hair from her face.

I didn't have a father—
like you do, César.

I listen:
Lucy's story of being alone.
Lucy's story of robed teachers with fierce cheekbones.
Lucy's story of impossible clocks and furious thick doors.

She uses the word *Sed*. Thirst.
She uses the word *Hambre*. Hunger.

Thirst.
Hunger.

I listen and scratch my elbow
until it bleeds.

Sister Martha closes the missal.
Says donuts and chocolate today,
after we finish the lessons.

Sister Martha warns me
to write only with my right hand.
The left hand is the devil's hand.
Glares at me. Hands me a box of chocolates
to sell in school. One dollar a bar, OK?
Warns me again.
At home, Lucy smiles.
Says both hands are good.
Gives me colors and a sketch pad. Imagine,
Lucy says. Imagine you are on a journey.

I draw a star and a moon. A lake glows
and weaves opal pools. A mountain wind
sways the leaves of a young tree.

Half in light, half in night.
My right hand is out in the open.
The left is hidden, a dark river
seeking light.

wirespeak

Thin moon up.
Midnight sleepy
on the sofa.

Wires speak——outside my apartment
rumble, melt: Wires keep everything tight——
telephone posts, cables, copper
undergrounds,

swelling
orange-eyed engines,

inside ferocious freeways, midnight malls
with plastic broom whirlers complaining at night:

Look out!
Ouch! Ouch!
They mesh, suck trash.

Electric TV webs
behind walls weaving unknown
jokes hidden from my ears.

Ha! Heeheeee,
they pulse.

The trees speak too,
their exotic leaves on the ground
form part of their story.

When it falls
rain says things to me.
Says
here,
hear,
here.

Everything
speaks.

I want to speak too. I purr to myself.
But when? How?

broken fingernails

El perro manda al gato, y el gato a su cola.
The dog bosses the cat, the cat its tail.

behind the target

Carlos Johnson laughs at my locker.
My poster of Selena. Bags of Cheerios.

A Mexican mad dogs me
as we pass the gym wall where we hang.

He's a new guy, I can tell because
Sammy invites him to ditch P.E.
next period. Nods yes, he nods
as if only Sammy can see him.

I can tell he's a tenth-grader, like me.
Mrs. Tinko's English class reader
on Julius Caesar. He's doggin' you, but
don't pay attention, homes,
says Carlos Johnson in his scratchy voice.

Mr. Santos's been checking you out
since you got into it with Xeng.
All the learning directors are on to you.
Carlos Johnson buzzes my ear.

Margarita with big eyes and long
trenzas[10] puts her arm around me.
Pulls me back to the lockers. Hey, Cees,
junior prom is coming up. You going?
Before I can answer, she's flying
toward the science trailers,
disappears.

What's a prom? Doesn't sound like
anything in Spanish. Maybe it's a fancy
BBQ with tuxedos. Prom?

Almost sounds like
promesa, a promise.

I open my locker. An arm shoots in
from behind, slams it shut. Jerks it
open.

My books fall out, pencils
and my lunch bag opens, pops and
spills on the floor. A burrito rolls
to Mrs. Tinko's open door.

The new guy in baggies, extra-large brown T
dogs me. Wazup with that?
I tell him picking up my lunch.

10. braids

Wazup is you, *cabrón!*[11]
He tells me screwing his mouth.
After school, behind Lucky's Mini-mart, *vato.*[12]
Be there! He struts away and slaps
Sammy, high-fives. They cackle
like *gallinas.*[13]

Alright,
I say to myself.

Está bien. I repeat. Cool,
cool, I say with fiery breath.

Kick my burrito away.
Peek into Mrs. Tinko's room.
Walk away. Ditch it.

i think about my father

Denver, the stiff snow,
formal as a shirt.

Ranchitos[14] in blue day smoke, mornings
rounding cattle. Weather so cold my mustache
turned into ice. His words, my father, César.

11. fool
12. dude
13. chickens
14. little ranches

I think about his jokes. The joke about
the three men: *calvo-man*[15] with his head
sizzling from the sun, *mocoso-man*[16]
with his nose melting.

And the *pulga-man*,[17] ribs roasting
with roaches. Laugh to myself, check to
feel my fuzzy mustache. Never screamed
at me. Never raised his voice. Maybe

once, when I hit Sonny, my buddy,
with a rock. I was just doing what
the other guys were doing. Bloody,
with his hands cupping his head,
Sonny forgave me. My father, mad.
Spun me in the air.

I think about his language of corn.
Milpa for corn patch, *atole* for corn meal,
maicito for tender young corn in your hand.

I move
to his slow walking style.

Chico,
he called me. Little first son.

15. bald man
16. runny-nose man
17. itchy man

Weighed five pounds, eleven ounces,
Lucy tells me. The doctor said, give him
fish oil so he can grow. Smelled like a trout.

Papi is fifteen years older than my mom.
We understand each other. She says. I wonder
how he feels about me. I wait.

I have *paciencia,*
like Lucy says.
My face gets long from waiting.

Holding a letter in my hand. A love letter
to my mom. My father writes, I wish I was
a cat, so that I could jump on your window
and say meow, meow. I can tell Lucy loves him.

I know he's coming back. He'll stay next time.
Each time he leaves us, he comes back sooner.

His name is César Benito. Named after his mother,
Benita. Born in a dusty village in Chihuahua.

My name
is his name. I know how to wait. I think
about my father, I work on the good things

then
I clench my teeth.

dance to selena

I disappear: into my mirrors.
At home. Turn on Selena. Accordions
glitter wild wings and ivory fangs. Dance to myself.
Push my feet back. Shoot my arms up.

Drop my face like a circus clown.
Alone now. Alone to breathe, sing.

Jiggle my hips to the snare drum beats.
Throw my head back. Spin, César.

No one is looking. Spin until you
melt. Into silver. Into diamond
streams. Come on, César, become
water, let your shoulders flow.

Go down into the floor, break
up the puzzle of the night. Go
swimming, go tumbling, spin
to the *tololoche*[18] snap of bass.

Slide to the other end. Raise
your hands. Spread your fingers
into starfish. Into the fuzz
waves, the rock blades, the reefs.

18. Mexican string instrument

The tidal waves come up. Your legs
rush into the green road of dreams.
Go there and tell Papi you ache.
Go there and unlock the songs.

See your mother in the kitchen.
Lucy pours *té de yerba buena*[19] to calm
her nerves. Mrs. Tinko is calling
you. Yes, you.
César, sing about *Canadá*

where it snows, where the waves
boil up emerald tigers. Wave
your hands—
spin into daylight.

erase everything
after school

School's out.
Walking with Miguel Tzotzil.
Cars rev. Couples giggle.
Mr. Bongosto, the principal, stands
facing the parking lot
like the Statue of Liberty, whispers
into Mr. Stanton's ear, the school cop.

19. spearmint tea

They gaze over the thin parades of students
weaving through flashy cars and mini-trucks.

Erase the silly talk. The snoring
in Mrs. Tinko's class. Erase
Mr. Wolf's history lecture about the Aztecs
and human sacrifice.

Aztecs showered themselves
in blood. Cannibals. He says. Margarita asks
Why? They wrote poetry too. Right?
He stumbles: Well, that's what they did
in those times, a war thing.

I don't understand,
Margarita mumbles and grows quiet.

Who can understand Mr. Wolf anyway
when he talks sideways, toward
the windows? Erase him.

Every time I breathe, I erase.
Erase the lockers full of burger trash
and glossy folders with phone numbers.
Erase the yearbooks that are too expensive,
that never show us leaning against the wall.
Erase, erase.

Jocks in red jeeps
ribbed tires
chrome bumpers. Erase.

Erase the English handouts on Shakespeare
that don't make sense and
the laughter in the front rows. The jokes
Mr. Wolf says to Timmy Montana and Mariah
Martínez, who get A's and get time on the computer.
Erase the front row. The second row too. Erase
all the words I imagine.

I am going down.
Behind Lucky's Mini-mart, next to
Western Wear. I can see Carlos Johnson
packing his '85 red Honda with six guys.

Sammy revs up his busted Camaro,
more guys and girls. Jammed inside.
Going to see me and the new guy fight.

We are the after-school stars
for this dry and empty sky,
this infinite afternoon.

broken fingernails

Miguel and I walk without saying a word.
We walk as if underwater,

as if we are dead leaves
or algae floating to the other
side of the shore. I can feel a wave from
behind about to suck me into its icy depths.

I am going down. Empty, sad
desert behind Lucky's Mini-mart.

The new guy circles me, his hands flapping
in front of him. Like fanning air into
his face—dark, head shaved.
He stares and burns his eyes.

The Mini-mart
is our basilica, dirt palace where our bodies
cross and go up in flames. New guy floats.

He is my altar. He is my mirror. I have
seen his face before—hard, glassy, reddish
eyes, his high cheekbones and his
tight lips, his small ears ready to track
any sound, a rain drop, a wisp of sand,
and his nose, thin, a bit hooked, his forehead
clean, smooth, blank.

29

He is sure——his shoulders
a small proud box in brown, long strides, he moves
like a cat, a dark spinning fur with eyes
that holler and growl and spark torches——
without a word, I can see Sammy in the circles
around us, I can see Miguel Tzotzil

and his tiny worried frame, he wrings his hands like towels
and Lulu, bowlegged in white overalls, jelly pumps
and Carlos Johnson, head phones on, quiet and

Maxy Ortega snarls,
hollers to the new guy——Kick his butt!
He's a *scrapa,* a wetback. Spits on me.

Swings and slams my nose,
he swings and I go down to the dirt, chokes me,
bashes my head against the ground,

I am drinking dirt and little pieces of wood,
my face is dragging against pebbles and rocks,
tears and hot blood and laughter, slapping hands,
high-fives and long stretched voices, cries, circle me

and my mother's face who knows crooked English and
my father's face who leaves me in a knot
and my empty living room back home and Mrs. Tinko
and Mr. Santos who don't speak Spanish
and Xeng who stomps on my new shoes

and my naked body that everyone sees—
in a veil of steam and shame

sprawled on the sand,
in the dark copper light.

Lulu lunges toward me.
Stop it man, it's over, alright
¡ya estuvo!, that's it,
she yells out.

Come on, *chavala*—
the new guy tears my shirt.
Let's finish it!

Jump back to the circle of hits, gravel bites, heat
and slams. Lulu pulls me back, hard.
Her black fingernails break off.

Maybe I am in my mother's womb, again
maybe, I am about to be born, about to die.
I am alone. My knuckles raw, face watery.

Everyone's gone.
Except Miguel Tzotzil.

Vámonos, César,[20] he pleads.
Pulls me up by my right arm.

Can't stop——the pounding, the broken alarms
in my heart.

requirements

I tell Lucy that I am sick
Run to my bed.

I tell her I am not hungry.
Curl up under the sarape.

I say don't look at me.
I say leave me alone.

I squeeze my face, bitten, scratched
swollen and cut, I squeeze and hope
she won't see me. Hope she won't
really see me. I am on fire as if someone
pulled off the skin from my face.

¿Qué te pasó? What happened to you?
She asks with her eyes
scared and full of tears. Touches my cheeks.
Nothing, I say. *Nada, mamá.* But
she is not here. I am pretending.

She's baby-sitting Mrs. Mata's six year old
a few blocks from here, on Chester Avenue.

She will come home late.
I'll leave her a note on the tiny TV.

Tomorrow. I'll tell Mama Lucy.
We had a wrestling match in P.E.

Requirements, I'll say—
for all tenth-graders.

walls & islands

Black kids sit by the food-vending machine.
Two perfect rows facing each other.

Jocks punch each other's shoulders
by Mr. Santos's office—I look out
across the recreation area at lunch time.

New guys with crooked hair cuts, loose shirts,
chew gum and spit. At the front of school.
Near the stage area, eucalyptus trees and short
brilliant lawns, in islands, girls walk by, holding
hands. Light tears across the flag pole.
Darkness swims in a pool by the lockers.

Hey, Sissyer,
how's it hangin'?

Sammy and Carlos Johnson call me.
Miguel Tzotzil follows. Mexicans
lean on the cafeteria wall.

Walk up.
Sammy pits

his finger into my chest. Jaibo, the new *vato*
jacked you up, huh? You're not a virgin
anymore. He says, chuckles—Look, you guys,
come on. He points across the yards.

Those Hmong dudes
think they're better than us.
Let's go.

I follow Carlos Johnson who follows Sammy.
Miguel Tzotzil strays behind and stops
by the water fountain.

Xeng and his guys lean against
the lockers in the math building. They
stare at Sammy, sway their arms,
clench fists.

Sammy and the *vatos* square off.
Xeng spits.

The fender inside my chest burns. Suck
the juice inside my mouth. Rub my metal chin.

The earth floor rocks. Bright. Waves
in my ears. My voice falls through the ground. Iron
in my seas. Mr. Santos appears. Jerks Sammy away.

Pulls me and Carlos Johnson. As we walk
up to the office, grabs Miguel Tzotzil. Leaves
us in the room with Mr. Stanton, the police.

OK, turn around. Hands behind your back.
Spread your legs—handcuffs Sammy, the tallest.

How do you say Raise your hands up, in Spanish?
He asks me. Don't know, I say in a low voice.

How about you, kid?
He asks Miguel Tzotzil.

Nothing from Miguel Tzotzil. I look out through
the window. The day burns the sky white.

Come on, you speak the language.
¿Se habla español? [21] You *Mexicano?*

Water comes down
Miguel Tzotzil's dark eyes.

fly into a sock

At Lucky's Mini-mart. Two blocks
from school. Rush into the toy section.
I hold up a model——'56 Chevy
like the one Papi drove away to Denver.
Red and white, the colors of apples
and milk.

Plastic watches, yo-yo's, lime green
see-through Uzi water guns.
Doll parts in bags. I take five
tubes of airplane glue, cup cakes and
a box of strawberry Pop Tarts.

Back at school, I give Sammy
two tubes, like he ordered. Sissyer,
he says, ready? I'm gonna show you
how to fly.

21. Wrong way of asking, "Do you speak Spanish?"

We go to the bathroom by the cafeteria
with Carlos Johnson and Maxy Ortega.

Sammy and Maxy pull out white gym
socks from a paper bag. Take one.

All you have to do is squeeze the tube
on the toe of the sock, just like tooth paste.
Roll it into a ball. And suck it, like a snow cone.

Feel it? Sammy says in a low voice.
Carlos and Maxy are in the toilets
with the paper bag smashed against their face.

In and out
in and out
in and out.

A cold wind, a heavy mint goes down
inside me, into my chest, it slides and
blows and gets warm, moves on its own,
a little body growing inside of me,

in and out
in and out
in and out

a dark
fish with one eye, swims up to my forehead
it is looking out through a green eye above
my nose, it does not think, it does not blink
the eel floats there, erect, stares, moves deeper
into my head, the tail curls around my bones.

In and out
in and out
in and out.

I want to fight it. The bag presses on my face
but I don't feel it. The little toilet fades and
waves. My head is down against my knees.
I can see my shoes and the blank tiles. Hear Sammy
and Carlos and Maxy walk out. Hear them shuffle.
Silence.

In and out
in and out
in and out.

César floats in front of the mirror. A jagged rock
is growing out of his forehead. His eyes are sleepy
and his nose is wet. There are no thoughts,
as he washes his hands, forgets to turn off the water.

No thoughts. No music.
Door opens——
a distant dreamy hand swishes
in the hot air.

In and out
in and out
in and out.

César is bent. His shirt is stiff, pants
droopy. César wipes his face again and again
on his way to his art class. Smiles.
César walks and cries and smiles.

and laughs
and laughs. Alone.

los heroes on f street

We're the last heroes, Sammy says
as we walk in a group with
beer and wine bottles in a bag
from Lucky's.

Everybody else is a *chavala.*
Everybody else is a wuss, wimps
on pogosticks. Nobody else but us.
Los Heroes!

Sammy and Maxy
say there's an empty *cantón*[22]
where we can go anytime.

Let's call it the Hero Shack,
Our place. Sammy cracks up.

We cross Chester Street, the main line,
La Reina Mexicatessen on the corner
where Doña Alvina makes *tortas de jamón con queso*[23]
for the *campesinos* that come into town
on payday, every Friday. They lean by their old
pickups with the Virgin Mary on the dashboard,
they talk and drink sodas
under the bitten eucalyptus tree.

Los Heroes dash behind the old Bekin's storage building,
on F Street, a tilted wooden shack with boarded
plywood on the door. Burnt and cut palm trees,
overgrown grass, weeds and spider webs.

A red tin
mailbox reads *Jenkins*——in broken
letters. We step through a busted
window on the porch. Enter
the dark rooms with shafts of sunlight
flickering on the floor.

22. house, pad
23. ham and cheese sandwiches

Those jocks are losers. Sammy says
as he lights up a cigarette. Wusses.
Yeah, Jaibo chimes in. *Chavalas.*

Those dorks in the front rows with
their hair that looks like somebody
spilled chocolate on their head—
losers. Maxy whistles and howls.

I check Jaibo. His skin is rough,
acne in patches and spotted bruises on his neck.
See him scratch his chin, how he drops
his eyes to the ground when he talks.

Black shirt, black pants. Buzzed head.
Like me. Like Maxy. Like all of us.
A shadow with long fingers. He could
almost play the piano.

Tough words,
copies Sammy. Jaibo about fifteen, my age.
Bigger. Could be my brother.

I always wanted an *hermano,* a brother.
Maybe that's why I don't know how to fight.

See Jaibo standing
next to Sammy. Another swig from the Forty.
Maxy squirts lemon juice into the bottle.

The shafts of sunlight rotate around the torn tiles
of the floor. There was a fire here.

Walls charred,
curled, a wire mattress with black antennas,
a sofa of ashes and singed wood.

Jaibo and Sammy slump to the kitchen, whisper
and unscrew another bottle, smoke, cough, laugh.
I mad dog Jaibo. But he's too drunk. Rub my nose,
feel the scabs on my forehead.

I pull out a bag of corn chips
watch light beams come down from
the caved-in roof. Up there, the trees sway
and the sky gathers its blue and green colors.

Up there, there is no fire, no burned doors, no small
shoulders leaning drunk against the sink, there
are no words up there, words that fall apart
that fade in glue socks, drown in amber red bottles.

Take a few steps toward the window. Look out
to the busted alley. My heart is barely beating. Sammy and
Jaibo, Maxy and Carlos Johnson huddle like sad candles.
Lean on each other as if searching for a spark.

I taste
ashes in my mouth. I taste a bitter sky
without light.

the scream in
mr. petrich's art class

Mr. Petrich points to a slide of Edvard Münch.
A charred bridge. Whirlpool sky, dead sea green
spins in liquid fire. Orange clouds.

Blast.
A face opens

in the fever-air. Moth face. The mouth
fades. Eyes without passengers. Skin wax, broom
heart. A figure of a woman who wants to scream.
She screams. No one can hear her.

Or
is it a man?
A boy?

The lines that circle her face
escape from her. Waves,
raw heat, the smell of burns and bones.

It is called "The Scream,"
Mr. Petrich says.

Turns to us
as we sketch with skinny charcoal
sticks. I draw Carolyn Center's face.
She's across the row. Just walked
into art class.

I had a bad batch, she whispers,
feel yellow. Her head goes down
on speckled newsprint sheets. Crank
makes her body drop.

Crank is the sea going to blue black.
Crank is the siren in Carolyn's head.
Crank is the bridge of promises on fire.

Carolyn drowns in a wreck of ashes
with her mouth asking
no questions. With her neck
sticking up, gloomy, a blond torch

tangled. Gone up.
Down fast.

drawing wires
across the page

Mr. Petrich hands me a sketchbook. Thanks me
for doing his daughter's homework—her Spanish class.

Watercolors in faded greens,
sharp red—blood red. Another page.

I take a charcoal stick and break it in half,
half and half again until I hold black ash.

Smear it with my open palm. Claw
the paper, jam my knuckles. Drag my fingertips
across the paper. Dark rain in night streaks.
A jungle blackened. A nightmare of arms cut off.

Swirl	black
rivers	wild
tempest	thick
no land	no island
no reef	no shore
no people	no leaves
no trees	no more.

Only deep carving
charcoal house charcoal face charcoal webs charcoal lace
charcoal bed charcoal mirrors charcoal suit charcoal weeds.

charcoal	walls
charcoal	falls
charcoal	charcoal
without	fire.

Spin my hand in fast circles
spin it, spin it. Spin away my arm
spin away my feet spin away my mouth that never speaks
spin spin into water into dirt into broken lonely hallways
spin into a dead dream of no sound and no colors. Disappear
César. You hear me in there, hey, you *chavala*, yeah

you Sissyer. What are you going to do?
What are you going to do about Jaibo *chavala?*
Are you going to let him beat you up?
In front of everybody hollering "You wuss!"
They are laughing at you *chavala*, can you hear them?
They are saying you are a *mojado*,[24] a sissy *mojado?*
A *scrapa*[25] from the south, Sissyer?
Where's your father? Good for nothing, right?
Where's your mother? You don't see her around here.
They would laugh louder if they saw her.
They would say,

24. wetback, derogatory term for undocumented worker
25. derogatory term for a person from Southern California, Mexico; wetback

look there goes Sissyer's mother
look at her droopy dress, look at her trying to speak
English. Look! You are a sorry *chavala,* man.

Are you going to sit here and cry or are you
going to get up take care of that Jaibo after school?
Says he's an *estrella,*[26] from El Norte, better than a *scrapa.*
He's your age, you know, he's going around
saying he slammed you. He's going around
strutting his stuff in front of Margarita. You know
you like her, come on. You even ditched so
you could walk to her house and wait for her
after classes. You better get it together Sissyer.
You better get on with it—*chavala.*

Camarón que se duerme
se lo lleva la corriente ...[27].

See this charcoal?
Take a good look.
See this grim dust?

You want to eat it?
You want to eat it?

26. star, a person from Northern California
27. Hurry up. Literally, "a sleepy shrimp gets taken by the wave."

seal boy

Mama Lucy watches "Fiesta Latina"
on the old TV box. Drinks coffee black
sings along with the dark eyes
of Olga Tañón.

You know, César, back in El Paso,
I almost joined a dance group, *Los Pirrines*,
but my older brother said it wasn't right.
Told your *mamá grande*, my mother, Dolores,
I would lose my way.

She takes a slow hot drink from her cup.
I wanted to be a dancer, César. On the stage,
just like Olga Tañón. See her?

I switch the channel while she goes to the bathroom.
A special on the "Circus Sideshows of America."
Families with bags of blue popcorn, hot can sodas.
Hot dogs with extra mustard and onions.

A "Sideshow" sign
on a shabby trailer.
SIDESHOW in fancy letters.
The S curly, the W wild.

Welcome to the Sideshow,
ladies and gentlemen,
the suited man with a cane and zebra hat says.
Come see The Bearded Lady, come see Lizard Man,
touch his skin, like alligator. Come one and all,
see The Sword Swallower, see the blade! Come now,
enter and you will see the double-headed goat
in a jar of whiskey. Come see The Fire Eater,
see Seal Boy, the boy that survives underwater,
a human kid with a fish-like face and
instead of arms, two shiny orange leather fins.
Welcome. Welcome.

Lizard Man
sits on a chair with a towel around his waist
and The Sword Swallower, next to him,
with his mouth that stretches slow,
his crooked throat and his right hand
raised above him with a long knife dangling
and the knife so serious, so pointed
slides down inside, teasing his heart.

I stare at the TV square. At nothing.
My head is full of changing light. In front
of the Seal Boy booth. Seen his face before.
His little whiskers painted
over his pink large mouth. The watery eyes.
wide and blinking and deep, searching
for the blue green light above. His front teeth
stick out, loose and almost pointed. No words
from his half-open mouth. His chest gray
and tender as if made of soap and tin. Dead
inside a thick jar of dirty vinegar and weeds.
His eyes swim toward me, almost speaking.

Back
to "Fiesta Latina"——Mariachis
strum in their tight gold-dust suits and liquid spurs.
Mama Lucy finishes the dishes. I stare
at Mama Lucy in the weak amber light of the kitchen,
moving her hands fast, stacking dishes, flapping the towel.
She turns slow motion to the tiny refrigerator. Leans
her head to one side as she smoothes the cold door.
Lucy, the dancer.

I gaze at my hard hands. Make fists, curl my fingers
tight, rub my hands together tight, turn them red red.

goldfish

Mrs. Tinko shows slides. She says London
and Yorkshire, Liverpool. The Beatles,
Rock and Roll. Shakespeare, Julius Caesar.
I raise my head from the table. César?

Carlos Johnson pokes me,
passes a large ink marker.

Says slip it under your arm, under your watch.
Open it Sissyer, he says, better than the sock!
Just put your head down, she'll think you are
taking notes or something.

No problemo, man.
Breathe it in. *Loco.*

Carlos Johnson sniffs from his shirt cuff too.
Breathe in, breathe out, boy

in and out
in and out,
that's it.

This is a story of a boy in search of his girl.
This is a story of a boy who can't cross the river.
This is a story of a girl who can't see the boy.
This is a story about how he loves her
This is a story about how she can't see him.
This is a story about how they must die.

In and out
in and out
in and out.

My nose is dotted with black ink
my shirt pocket has a pool of black blood stains.

The bell rings and I stumble.
Bow my head and rush out the green wooden door.
Jaibo shoots his arms into the air playing like
a rebound by Michael Jordan. Across the hall.
Sammy shoots a three-pointer. Pretends.

Whoosh!
Whoosh!

I push Jaibo into the lockers, against his face.
Why don't you rebound this? Kick him.
Why don't you rebound this? Slam his head
Why don't you ...

Mr. Stanton, the school cop,
grabs me from behind.

I smile through a glassy mask,
my face is wild. Legs bowed, bent.

Get up, loser,
come on let's ...
My mouth moves.
I wipe my nose.

Mr. Stanton pulls me, hand cuffs me.
Walkie talkie in hand, Mr. Santos pushes students away.
Takes Jaibo. I see Margarita, cringing, her books
against her face.

I give her a cool look,
my eyes fade. Under water——students
wiggle and erase.

You're high, Garcia. What's the matter with you?
Mr. Stanton looks into my eyes, my shirt, the marker
with its broken nose spilling. You are in big trouble.

Drags me.
Limp legs, charged head.

In the office
bent over. My left eye feels bigger
than my right eye. The doorknob
has my face in it. Spots on my cheeks,
my orange gold face. Giggle. I smile
in a dirty gold bubble. I smile a sad smile.

What did I do?
I mumble to Mr. Stanton, my teeth out.
What did I do?

captain krunch

At home for three weeks, suspended.
One more time, you go to Sunway Continuation.
I can hear Mr. Santos's voice. Over and over.

Mama Lucy is out baby-sitting. Told her
Go to Lucky's, get me some comic books
and a box of Captain Krunch.

TV on. Soaps in Spanish. Go to my room, blast
Selena, some rap and *Sangre India,*[28]
a Mexican CD Miguel Tzotzil lent me.

Laugh into the mirror,
at the stack of homework makeups
on the carpet.

Take a needle from my mother's
red pin cushion by her bed. Burn it over
a *veladora*[29] for the Virgin Mary

Poke an X
over my right arm, rub ink.

X is the target.
X is my two fists flying.
X is me alone, sailing in the hall.

X is two days to go
and then, back to school.
X is two wires against each other.

X is me kissing Margarita.
X is nothing I know.
X is a broken question mark.

My arm bleeds. Wipe it off
with a paper towel. Alcohol
smoothes it out. Every stitch

is a silent word in my head.
Every stitch is a day in the back row.

Push the blood back with the ink.
Red & Black——colors of rage
and shade.

29. prayer candle

Ink and skin.
Fists and night.

Back at Rambling West. Almost two o'clock.
In my history class. Mr. Wolf
talks sideways, to the trees outside the window.
Saying something about Teddy Roosevelt
and the Rough Riders.

Sammy laughs, shoots a spit wad.
No one listens.

I am going round and round.
X with nowhere to go.

X
X
X
With nowhere
to go.

kmart specials

Hey chavala!
Yeah, you!
Wanna do something?
Better than selling
those *chavala* chocolate bars.

Sammy yells across the street,
from Lucky's Mini-mart. Maxy Ortega
smokes and spits next to him. Hide the chocolates
in my hip pocket. Mama Lucy says
I've got to try. Do something positive.

Mira,[30] man, Sammy puffs into my face.
We need you to be our lookout.
Easy as 1–2–3.

Easy as
A
B
C
Maxy chimes in with a hard, angry
sad look.

Just look out for *la jura.*[31] Maxy and me
are going to score some key chains and stuff.
When we come out, you let us know
if it's clear. If not we'll dump the stuff.

Come on, man.
¡La hacemos![32]
¡Los Heroes!

30. Look!
31. the police
32. Let's jam! We can do it!

Sammy slaps me on the back and offers
me a cigarette. Save it for later.
We'll go to our shack,
have a real good time. Someacidtoo.
He says it all fast.

Be cool now,
he says, grinning and stepping
into Kmart. I am outside by the rocking horse.
The sky is clear today, the sun burns
on all the little cars in the lot. Mothers and
baby carriages. Two guys with CDs.

We never come here. We go to Western Wear
when they have specials, or National Dollar in Logan
Lakes, a few hours away. Most of the time
we go to the Good Will by our house.

Sammy and Maxy step up to the glass door,
arms crossed over their puffy shirts.

I throw my hand up and nod my head to one side.
Everything's cool, I whisper.

As soon as they step outside, Sammy yells, Run, *loco!*
I keep on walking. Sammy shoots down the street
and Maxy follows. I keep on walking, faster and
faster. Wait here a minute, young man!

A cop
grabs me by the shoulder.
Cuffs my wrists behind my back.

I look at him with tears in my eyes.
You were with those boys, right?
I tell him I didn't know
that they were stealing shirts.

Look, if you didn't do anything
you don't have to worry.
You know where they live?
No, I tell him.

The store detective next to him stares at me,
at the X on my arm.

You go to Rambling West High?
I know where to find you. He says
squeezing my arms, scanning my clothes,
my face, the scabs on my nose.

They'll come back. He tells the cop who
pops open the silver cuffs behind my back.
I bust 'em everyday. I'll be looking for
this one, Mr. X.

I don't want this. I tell myself.
Everyday, I get further and further
from home, from school.
How do I get back?

The cop car purrs to my left, follows
me down the street and parks ahead of me.
Stops me. Look Mexican, I know you have a record!
Where's your father? Is he like you? Don't tell me.
You're all alone, right? Like the rest of us.
Get off my streets. Got it?

Nod yeah. Yeah. Got it. Got it.
Walk away, slow style. Little houses,
tiny trees in the solar blaze.

Pass Maxy and Sammy who guzzle beers
in the old shack. In the burned house.
Punch each other in the arms.
In the house without a *familia.*[33]

Walk away. Walk away, César.
My arms hurt. Wrists burn. Breathe, boy.
Turn back, run home.

culture night at rambling west

Culture Night—
Mama Lucy says *vamos.*

Maybe I'll get to know the teachers. You too.
She tells me, with her warm hand on my shoulder.

Your grades, no more fights, OK?
¡Me vas a sacar canas verdes![34]
You know?

You can do it.
She pats me on my head.
Sí se puede, you can do it!
Lucy cheers into my ear,
sings and hurries to shut off the little stove.

Think about the choices you make,
she tells me.

Mr. Stanton passes out punch, in police
attire, in strict blues. Mr. Santos, our vice-principal
slaps his hands together as he welcomes the parents.

---

34. You're going to give me green-gray hairs!

Xeng and his mom dressed with a flowery
scarf sit with us. Three Mexican parents
and Xeng's mom. We float around
the cafeteria. Weak lights flicker above us.

Red napkins twisted
on the long brown cafeteria table.

Ginger cookies, steel drums of coffee, watery tea.
Mr. Stanton clicks on a slide show. Talks gangs—
how to identify students in trouble.

Underwear pulled up, he says.
Look for the colors.

Colors for south,
colors for north.

The numbers:
check the numbers, he repeats, maybe 13's,
maybe 14's—tattoos on the neck,
with animal faces. He stares at me.

Daggers, crosses and skulls. Hand-pumped needle
scars, branding iron burns, welts and words.

Don't forget the words—codes, secret languages.
Mr. Stanton's eyes sparkle, his starchy voice

bounces over the empty seats. Lucy and I
gaze at each other, at Xeng and his little mom.
Little like Lucy, Xeng's mom pleads,

Do what you have to, please,
tell us what to do. The slide machine jerks
to a stop. I rub my arm.

There are question marks
burning in the coffee, on Mr. Stanton's face too.

Mr. Santos is quiet. Tells Xeng's mom,
We appreciate your support.

We answer
with our bodies.

Some of us go south, others north.
The rest disappear into the night.

the deer & the jaguar

Don't know what to do. At home. In my old jacket,
curl myself into a chrome ball on the sofa. Listen
to *Rock en Español.*[35]

Gray chalk
circles around my eyes.

35. Mexican rock and roll in Spanish

Miguel Tzotzil's on the E-Z chair,
a squeaky elf with *huaraches.*[36] TV on.

No sound.
Eat a hard *bolillo*[37] with butter.

You know, César. Miguel Tzotzil begins,
We are on the earth's surface.

What?
The earth's surface——Miguel Tzotzil repeats
with a quiet and big voice——is the world
of trouble, bad troubles between friends and families.
There is another side.

Do you know
your animal companion? He asks me.
Mine is the deer. At night, my ancestors feed it
in the corral of Great Mountain, back
in Chiapas. The deer grazes the grasses,
runs free. If I hurt someone, or lose
sight of my family, the deer breaks
off from safety in Great Mountain.
The deer is abandoned. Dies.
I am abandoned, like an orphan.

36. leather sandals
37. bread roll

I don't believe in all that stuff. I tell him
as I curl into a tiny piece of steel.
Turn up the hot music in my ears.

Your companion is calling you.
He says. A baby jaguar howls at the moon.

A tender, young jaguar,
of the blue green forest. Alone, he
will grow cold.

You
must bring him back into the corral.
You must carry him back to Great Mountain.

He will grow strong, his voice
will be like thunder. Bring him back, César.

Blue and red flashes from the TV screen
erase and mix our faces.
Miguel Tzotzil's eyes are my eyes.

The music spins. My jacket
comes to life in new spotted colors,
the paws swish through wet trees,
winds on the green river.

Where is Great Mountain?
How do I get there?
Jaguar boy,
can you hear me?

sammy flies over the fence

The baseball diamond is a rough brick of dust.
Almost bloody. Shadows rip across the lawn.

I am in the library drawing
cartoons, instead of algebra. A square plus
B square equals C square. What is A?

Miguel Tzotzil scrambles to my table.
¡Mira! he says—the fence! Sammy, Maxy and
guys from the Westside.

¡Mira! They are jumping over, flying
with bats. Duct-taped sticks. They're chasing
Rigoberto, the new Mexicano.

Sammy yells, Don't you ever call me a wetback,
and swings. Hits the boy on the nose,
slams him again. I am seeing things

through a Coke bottle. Everyone melts, screams.
Everyone in twists of arms, fast bodies at odd angles.
Bloody hands, and dresses. Ragged shirts
and swollen marbles on foreheads. Upside
down skies, Carlos Johnson

on the pavement scrambling,
looking up. Mr. Stanton's foot on his back.

My hands shrink, stomach jangles. White light,
my heart is lost, the feet I have are stupid.
Fall into a pit, the hidden waves
from the bottom of the school. They rise up
snap at my feet like wild wiry seals.

Sammy is cuffed,
his face smashed against
peppery sand.

Mr. Stanton on his walkie-talkie. Sammy
lays there, curled, muffled shrieks,
on the concrete floors by the cafeteria.

He moves his mouth but no one can hear him.
He wants to spell his name with his body
but no one knows or cares.

one block west of the
st. james retirement hotel

Miguel Tzotzil, Mama Lucy and I stroll
downtown Fowlerville. Pass the Eagle Pawn shop.
Walker's Western Wear. We stop

at J.Z. Jewelry. Lucy breathes on the window,
between her and a zircon ring. The emerald necklace.
Esmeralda, she says so that I won't forget my Spanish.

Your father's birthstone is in February,
she tells me. I think of Denver.
Canada snow. Tidal waves in Nova Scotia—
a tiny town engraved green by the ocean.

Miguel mentions his father, Mikel,
as we stop in front of Apex Music.
He's a salt seller in the *mercados.*[38]

Once there was a famine in our *pueblo,*
he told me. Banana roots, lemonade,
fern roots, a few *tortillas.* Dinner.

All the corn
was gone.

38. open-air markets

People who don't know corn, they
step on it. They toss corn cobs
half eaten. Corn is holy. Papi Mikel says.

I remember planting corn too
with my father. In *ranchitos*. Outside, in the fields,
dropping yellow pearls into rough
hollows I made with my finger.

We stare through the window.
A saxophone sparkles
in an open burgundy velvet cradle.
A miniature curled cat of gold fur—
a bell mouth with a mystery
voice hollers at me.

Stare.
Miguel and I move our hands fast
in front of our puckered mouths.
We play hard. We imagine our music.

We dance for a second. Our fingers fly like angels,
tap invisible keys on our faded cotton shirts.

from stones to water

Carlos Johnson and me. Ditch school.
Eat Ho-Hos, guzzle sodas. Chew gum
at the same time. Laugh out loud
and throw stones at dogs.

Sit outside
Lucky's Mini-mart, listen to fast noise.

Sammy's at Sunway Continuation, he tells
me, rubbing his head. You too? I ask him. Yeah, man.
Pokes his nose and cleans his hand on his pants.

I look at Miguel Tzotzil across
the street, going home, after school
with a bag of potato chips.

Come on, Sissyer! Are you with us
or are you a *chavala?*

Let's get that Indian!
Carlos Johnson spits and elbows me.

The word Indian rings in my ears. Sounds
like Mexican, except it's smaller, dirtier.

No one says they are Indian.
No one says *indio.*

What am I?
Mama Lucy says she's Indian. I think
she's joking.

You get him from behind and I'll get him
up ahead——I'll sneak up on him. I stall.
Carlos Johnson pinches my nipple and
slams my shoulder with his fist:

Wazup,
Sissyer?

You think you're better than us?
You think you are like the rest?
You think we are the losers?
You think you are an Honors *chavala?*
You wanna hang out with the *indio?*

Why does indio = getting hassled with no one to protect
you?
*Why does indio = graduating from school not knowing
English?*
*Why does indio = nothing, maybe just a scrap, trash, un
scrapa?*

Why does Mama Lucy say,
Soy india?[39]

If you back out, I'm gonna tell Sammy,
I'll tell Maxy. We'll just tap him, come on!

I bow my head
walk slow behind Miguel Tzotzil.

Carlos Johnson crouches behind a van
on the right, half a block ahead.

Pick up rocks
by the road. Clean, smooth, hot
sharp pieces. Stuff them into my pockets.

I don't know if I am breathing.
I don't know if I am walking or floating.
I don't know if I am following Miguel Tzotzil
or my own shadow,

the one that used to tremble
the first days of school, the one that used to cry
underneath the stairs while class was going on.

Cars race by.
I don't hear them.

39. I am an Indian woman.

All I hear
is a rain sound inside my head, a cellophane
sheet stretch and pop. Fire twisting
sparks, slivers of glass chipping off.

Two rocks in my left hand.
One in my right. I swing my left arm
look ahead at the tiny target.

Maybe Miguel Tzotzil will join us
after we jump him. Maybe he'll be
one of us. Yeah, that's right, just maybe.

Carlos throws a small stone.
I can see it arc across Chester Street,
an upside down C. A stone mouth
about to bite flesh.

Miguel Tzotzil runs,
drops books. Drop chips.

I launch three rocks as hard as I can,
one after the other, with my eyes closed.
Faking it. Hoping they will burn away in the sky.

Open my eyes,
slow walk, in a dream, almost:

Little Miguel Tzotzil, my friend,
on his side, his head bleeds, face screams. I duck
but he sees me, calls me—

¡César! ¡César!
¡Ayúdame! Help Me!
¡Ayúdame, César!

Run with Carlos Johnson.
Run as fast as I can. Pass the La Reina Mexicatessen.
Don't look back. I don't understand Spanish, right?
No one speaks Spanish here, in Fowlerville.

Run, run,
run until all I can see
is a red brick wall. Blank wall.
Blank face. Blank sky.

The sidewalk is a snake.
I am riding it. Swivels and jerks
and leaves me at the thorny gate.
Inside the Hero Shack.

Old beer bottles choked with cigarette
butts, others with urine. No one.

Steely palm trees
and broken bed springs. In the kitchen
window, a spider maneuvers
its long legs, tilts its shrunken head and
pinches the belly of a fly.

All right, dude! Carlos yells crazy
and hands me a pack of peanut-butter cookies.
You did it. Cool, man. When I tell Sammy,
just wait, he's going to crack up, man.

I think of tomorrow:
Mr. Santos will call me in. I know it.
He will come into Mrs. Tinko's
first period. Wait at the door. It will be around
eight thirty, just enough time to check the rosters,
have a cup of coffee, announce
track competitions for the week's end.

Mrs. Tinko will say,
You are excused, Cesar. Mr. Santos would like
to see you now. You can leave your stuff
on your desk.

I'll get up, look
as if I am going to get an award,
I'll even grin,
say, Check you later, to Margarita.

I am sorry
but we don't tolerate this kind of behavior.
Mr. Santos will say this looking at me through
his gold-rimmed glasses. I am sorry, he'll
repeat it, shaking his head in his scented office.

Ever since you came to Rambling West High
you've been in trouble. Your grades,
your attitude. You know what, Garcia?
Mr. Petrich's art class
is the only class where you even got a C!

Mr. Santos will remember me and my mom
at Culture Night. He'll remember Xeng
and Xeng's mom and how he didn't know
what to do with us. How Mr. Stanton, the
school cop, described gangs and tattoos and
other dangerous things at school.

Mr. Santos will look at my arm, at my X.
He will shake his head again. A few more words:

Miguel Tzotzil didn't want to tell me
it was you. But when I warned him
that I was going to call his parents,
he told me—

César did it.
    It was César.
        César García!

That will be the first and last time
he says my full name. And I will feel
a sense of pride, almost. I will feel that whatever
I came to do at Rambling West, I accomplished it
in that one moment when Mr. Santos
said my name—*César García.*

Then he'll pull up his pant legs, like
he always does when he sits in his leather chair
next to his desk with photos of his wife
and his three children dressed in suits.

Mr. Santos will pronounce his words
like Mrs. Tinko wants us to, his lips and tongue
will sound smart and tidy.
"As of tomorrow, you, Mr. Garcia, are going
to Sunway Continuation. Some of your friends
are there already."

He will make a call. Cross his legs,
look at his shiny black laced shoes as he talks.
Sign papers.

I curl my fists into sharp springs. Tighten my face.
Walk behind him, with hard shoes. Breathe hard.
I am leaving Rambling West.

When I move my eyes across the cafeteria,
when I pass by Mr. Wolf's room, where he's barking out
the assignment on the chalkboard,
every face makes me laugh inside. Every
page that turns registers in my ears.

What are they reading? Who discovered America?
Who is Fernando Cortés? Did Cortés hate Moctezuma?
What were Cuauhtemoc's last words?

I will see my father's way of walking
as I notice Mr. Santos, how he drags
one foot a little more than the other.

My father didn't say goodbye
when he left,
he just left.

Empty my locker. Tear up
Selena's poster. Mr. Santos next to me,
with my books. I am grinning
crazy like Carlos Johnson and Sammy.

Follow Mr. Santos through the halls again,
past the football trophies
to the front door facing the street.

Miguel Tzotzil stares at me from his room.
I can't see him, but I can feel his eyes. His deer eyes.
I can hear his deer hooves running free
in the blue night pastures of Great Mountain.

Miguel, where am I running to?
Can you hear me? I am sorry Miguel
but I had to do it.

Perdóname, Miguel,
I whisper in Spanish.
Forgive me.

Mr. Santos gives me an envelope,
says to take it to the main office at Sunway. Crosses
his arms by the door.

Spit to one side when I get out.
No more tears. Nothing.

My father didn't say goodbye.
He didn't say a word. He just left me
and my mother one Thursday night
on the last week of July. I don't cry
like I used to. Nothing like that.

There will be water coming down my cheeks
as I pass Lucky's, as I walk with hard legs and baggies,
past Chester Street, as I see my apartment building
next to Bradley's Burgers. My door: gray door
with the number 9 by the peep hole.

There will be water
rushing from the deep. Down my face.
That's all. Water. Then night.

hanging in space

El pez por su boca muere.
A fish dies by its mouth.

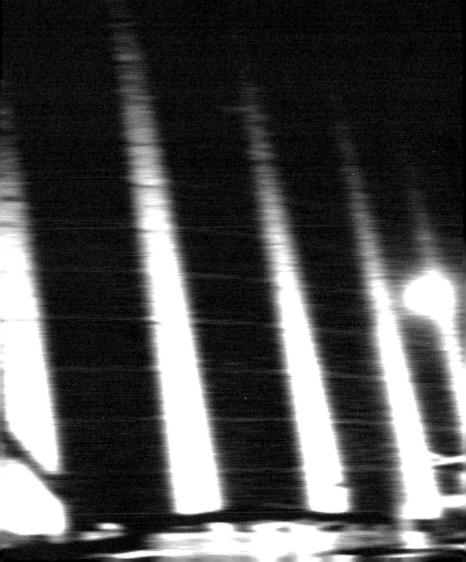

2 x 43

Two o'clock. Morning.
Can't sleep. Rub my hands against my face.
Feverish. On the dark sofa.

Press my face
against the cool window glass.
Bradley's Burgers flashes neon hula
hoops around a giant sloppy burger
in the silvery sky.

I cough.
My eyes burn and the moon spills a weak
light on our splintered brown floor.

When we first arrived in Fowlerville
Papi César said, *Vamos a lonchar.*
Took me and Mama Lucy to Bradley's.
Vamos a celebrar. Celebrate, he said.
His cheeks pink. His mustache bright.
Then, a cloud over his face.

He spoke of his diabetes. His legs.
Sometimes I can't feel my feet,
Papi said, kicking up his dusty Stacy
Adams shoes. I sipped
a chocolate malt.

Diabetes? *Chale.*
I don't care, he said.
He picked up a little shiny
square pack from the plastic orange table.

Next to the salt. See
this grape jelly?
Watch me. He popped it open
and sucked out the thick jelly.

I can eat all the sugar I want.
Una vez al año. Once a year.
A little sweetness won't hurt you.

Mama Lucy pushed
his hand away from his mouth.
¡La diabetes, César! ¡Ya no! No more!

Papi looks
into my eyes. For a second or two.
Breathes in. Breathes out, says,
You are a smart *muchacho.*

Every month I send
thirty *dólares*[40] to a company in Arizona.
Five acres of *pura tierra.*[41]
Just for you, César. Exhales.
Inhales slow. His eyes water as if
he already knows he is leaving.
Quickly turns
to Mama Lucy.

If they chop off my legs, he says
with a nervous laugh,
I'll make my own out of 2 x 4s!
Right, César?
Slaps me on the shoulder.
Right?

Papi fades away
in the circles of neon.

What would I tell him?
Where? Walking?
When? Home? What land?
Whose *casa?* Wha . . .

40. dollars
41. pure land

All I have
are half words. Torn
words. They heat up
in the night.
They dangle and sizzle
inside of me.
They drop deep
and break apart,
melt.

I can still hear Papi's footsteps
the night he left. Hear him
drag his left foot
slower than his right.

I smooth my forehead
with my hand. Am I
a smart *muchacho?*
Am I?

I scratch the side of my face,
gaze at the moon. I can see
the broken glass
on its face. Gray sharp
patches on its tender skin,
feel its hot silver mouth.

Tomorrow I step
into Sunway Continuation.
César, el smart muchacho,
I say to myself breathing hard.
Close my eyes.

Night covers me
with its blanket of electric blue wool.

orientation

1. Papeles

Cross town
to Sunway Continuation.
Get off the bus,
number 13. Eight A.M.

Mama Lucy said—
Pórtate bien, behave yourself.

Mama Lucy said—
Que dios te bendiga,
may God bless you.
I stare back.

Mama Lucy blesses me with her right hand,
the sign of the cross on my forehead.
As she prays, I stare at her eyes, the
way I have since I was child. Standing
in front of her, listening to her words,
I look into her and listen to a river stream,
a kindness I have never heard anywhere else;
I can almost see the waters, I can hear the music—
it is sweet and fragrant. I am safe for a second,
the stars of the night follow me during the day
I can smell her perfume, the sweet kind she buys
at Lucky's. Then her small tender hand
and a thin wedding band fade away.
I step onto the curb, bus door slams,
the wind churns and I am a stranger once again.

Wear my baggies, gray, and my hat,
black. Hands in my pocket, I check into
Sunway. A few faded beige buildings
on the corner of Dakota Street. A sloppy
fence and a dirt yard.

Sign reads:
"This is a drug-free zone."
Bear flag flaps, above me, curls and snaps.

Inside, secretary Yolanda Davies, her name
on a giant green plastic holder,
bites a maple bar, pauses and asks me for my papers.

¿Papeles?
Papers?

Papers? Remember stepping off
the bus in Las Cruces for the chile-picking season.
Mama Lucy with her colored jute bag and her
brown purse full of oranges. Man with
a green hat said, *¿Papeles?*

Man in a green hat and green shirt and pants
said:

Papers?
Passport?

Bite my lip
show Mrs. Davies my papers.
I can tell this is a small school.
Shrunken buildings and tiny halls
the baseball diamond
makes me laugh.

Hey there, Daniel, Ms. Davies says
to a guy behind me. He mad dogs me
and swishes away.

You'll have to go to orientation-
four weeks. If you miss one day
you have to start over again, she tells me
in a tough-man voice
as she takes another bite
from the maple bar with a custard center.

Orientation, I say to myself:
Another word that means nothing.
Another word to blow away.

2. Snack Bar

Just out of second period.
Go to the "Lunch Box," a tiny closet
where an old thin white man sells chips,
sandwiches and sodas.
Students sit around
twelve dark benches. Tight groups
and slow words.

Daniel hangs
with three *vatos.* Hear him:

I had a fool in my class, see
that dude we seen in the office. He's kind of weak.
Let's hit him up, see what he's down with.

He says this with his back to me.
I take a Twinkie and a Coke. Sit a bench away.
Sammy and Carlos Johnson squat low
by a bulletin board in the front. Dark
glasses. Nod their heads, chew gum
check the girls out.

Daniel pushes a short guy they call Little John.
Yeah, you. Let's see what you're all about.
Gets pushed again. Haven't seen you
in the hood lately. Daniel whispers into his ear
as he looks at me from the side.

Later with this oil and imitation
cheese sandwich, Little John says,
and passes by me pretending
I am just another guy
at the snack bar. Just another guy
visiting this hard blue square of Mexicans
Blacks, a few Asians, a handful of whites.

3. Circles of Fire

Bus number 13. First week.
Say it as I pull out and read
Mama Lucy's directions to school
on a shredded piece of paper.
Thirteen, that means good luck.
I laugh.

Squeeze and chew the paper.
Spit it into Dakota Street. Someone's hands
press around my eyes. Guess who it is?

Uh, uh … Margarita?
Geez, no way, Cees. It's me.
Guess again.

I don't know, I wheeze. Mom?
Yeah right!

Pull the hands off my face
turn around. Carolyn Centers
is laughing, the ring on her eyebrow flips up
then she puts her hand across her mouth.
Black blouse and short brown
skirt flapping.

What are you doing here?
I ask her with my eyes as round as donuts.
Shhh, nevermind, she says. Busted for dope.
Shhhh.

Her face loses its color. Comes up
to me and whispers: They are getting loaded
on weed behind the bleachers. My homies
say Little John is going to do a hit on you,
see what you are all about.

Going down fast. Again. First week
and I am out of orbit. First week
and the world is a trap.
New bell schedule, new charts.

My new teacher, Ms. Steiger, wears sixties clothes,
mirrors on her motorcycle jacket. Long rainbow skirt.

Erase all the talk about self-esteem they gave me
at orientation, erase respect, erase the word cooperation.

Erase the icebreaker:

Old and new students please form a circle.

Hold hands and huddle as tightly as you can,
Ms. Steiger said. If you want to get inside
the circle you have to break in, do not expect
people to let you in nice and easy. You've got
to push and make yourself known. Come on,
César, try. Everyone else has.

Push in with my head, with my arms, an elbow,
push in with my knees—against their knees,
pry open the door, kick the wall down, don't say
please, don't cry by the stairs, come on, César, push
get in there, with your head, smash your face
through their arms, bust in, scream out,
get in, scream out and shoot through the rock,
the steel bulb, the knot of arms against you.
Go!

I was on the floor, swimming almost, sweating,
pushing, almost shouting, until I just ran into them,
went through.

Now get inside, César. Ms. Steiger says as she plays
with a turquoise locket hanging from her neck.

Alone,
inside.

This time you have to break out of the circle.
This time you have to push out, I don't know
how you are going to do it, everyone has their own way,
count to three and you have fifteen seconds to get out:

1
2
3
   Go!

I can hear the numbers. I can feel the bodies
of these new guys, Cheyenne, Quintana and Barlow.
Sammy and Carlos Johnson are in the circle too.
They have been here for a semester already. They laugh
and act like they don't know me. They press
against me like slow tractors. Sammy dogged me
when I ran in, wants me inside, he wants me to
lose myself inside the circle, to stay inside
with him and Carlos Johnson, he doesn't want
me out,

no one wants me out.
I am the new guy again, the stranger that always
falls back
to the beginning.

Nothing has changed, I am sitting at the stairs on the first
day of class at Rambling West High, I am being tested over
and over again, spinning in a wire wheel circle of blows
without end.

The circle is what my father left me——his distant hand
The circle is what my language left me——its accent of shame
The circle is what I have inside——a terrible scream
The circle is the rule of the house——thirst and hunger
The circle is called by another name——welcome boy, *scrapa!*
The circle is my clock, my heart——my silence in red.

I am fooling myself with words.
The circle is nothing.

1
  2
    3
       Go!

Run toward Sammy and Carlos Johnson
brothers by accident, brothers by crushed arms against
each other, by hard eyes of fury against the unknown.

See myself running inside the circle, going forward
head first, arms out as if to be born, into the darkness

toward Carolyn, toward Ms. Steiger on the outside
with my eyes and teeth on fire. With my face going
from red red to blue green wind.

paganini & hawaii

Ms. Steiger comes up to my oval desk.
Sammy and Carolyn work at their assignments
on sentence structure. See this?

Ms. Steiger says, holding up
an worn, honey-colored violin.

A Stradivarius can call the spirits,
she says, pacing to the front.

Paganini was a wild man. The few
that dared to play his music went crazy.
You, in the back! She calls me.

You, what's your name again? Yes, you.
César, I squeak.

Full name?
Uh, César García. I say
as an ancient dynamo begins to whirl
metal wicks inside my chest.

García, what do we call this?
She plucks the strings. Wants me to name
the term for plucking strings.

I open
my mouth full of fishes and dangerous
wires snapping. García?

Pizzicato. I squeak, my neck flutters.
My mouth is screwed. Good, she says.

She mentions Heifetz, Isaac Stern.
Passes the violin to me. Show it
to Sammy who sits next to me.

Pizza-taco! Sammy barks
and punches my shoulder.

Ms. Steiger turns to me. Walks over
through the tiny desks. César,
she says. You have a good ear.

She says to me. Moves to Sammy.
Steps close and whispers to him:
Pizzicato, Luna. *Pizzicato!*

By the way, García, what are you?
You pronounce Italian so well.

I shrink. Crumble into my chair.
The violin is a huge beetle of burned
shells in my left hand. A spider's prey, a moth
with spotted chalk wings.

Hawaiian! I say quickly. Hawaiian,
Ms. Steiger! The word *Mexican*

is an evil eel,
a lost serpent in my throat.

No one says Mexican in class. I'll lose
my voice if I say it.

become an oboe

Third-week progress reports:
Ms. Steiger gives me a B-
I freeze in the back row. A note
at the bottom of the slip. *Let's form
a band or a choir by the end of the semester!*

A choir? I sink into my seat
as Sammy walks in late.

Shut up, or I'll tell Ms. Steiger
you wrote Carlos Johnson's paper
on Bach for him! He says.

I wrote your paper too. I squeak.
Sammy puts his head down
on his desk and goes to sleep.

Ms. Steiger slips an album
over an old wiry phonograph box, says,
Become oboes! Become!

Listen to the double reeds, she says.

Put your hands up in the air
sing out your names
wave your arms, she says with her hands
moving, almost swimming upward to the sky.

Carolyn waves
and sings out her name, giggles and laughs
until tears roll down her eyes.
Talks about fugues
and Mozart's brain. I slump
and frown.

Sammy snores.
I bend my body forward,
raise my hand. Maybe
I can borrow the violin,
I say to Sammy. Wake him.

Slam! Slam!
Sammy punches me.
Asks me, Is it lunch time?
It's only 10:15. Sammy is always
hungry.

So am I.

cantatas in the morning

6:17 A.M. In our Westside apartment
I sleep on the old brown leather sofa.

Someone is knocking. Mama Lucy says.
Mr. Chalmers, our social worker, peeks
between the door and bronze chain.

Lucy whispers, "He's checking
to see if anyone is living with us
who is not on the *Huero Félix*[42] forms."

Carita de santo
los hechos no tanto.

He has the face of a saint
but his actions saintly ain't.

42. A phonetic wordplay on the term welfare—"werofary." "Werofary" becomes a funny blonde character called "el Huero Felix," the Blonde Felix.

Get up.
Put on my head phones. Brush my teeth
while Mama Lucy escorts Mr. Chalmers
through the kitchen. Ba-ba-baba-baah, I sing,
waving my arms up, my double reeds.

What are you listening to? he asks me.
Johann Sebastian Bach, I tell him. Wha?

Cantatas, I say. Mr. Chalmers opens
his mouth as if to bite a stolen pear.

Cantatas, I repeat. Cantataahs!
Like *cantadas* in Spanish. Like
things sung out in the open, I say
louder than I need to.

Mr. Chalmers nods his head.
Cantadahs? OK ... OK ... Leaves.

blue fire

Drop my head. Tell Ms. Steiger
I am not interested in being in a band.
Sammy said it's for *chavalas!*

Too bad, she says. You can play
anything. You know how a clarinet
sings, a French horn, a piccolo.

I chuckle. Piccolo sounds like
lo picó in Spanish. *He got bit.*

Remember? she asks.
Your Beethoven essay assignment?

Remember how Beethoven went deaf?
And then composed what he could
not hear? My eyebrows make
upside down shapes. Yeah, yeah.

He could hear everything inside,
I say. Squirm and cover my mouth
after I speak. So do you, Ms. Steiger says.

I leave her leaning on the chalkboard
with Sammy working on pronouns.

Stroll out
thinking about wild Beethoven.

See him smash notes on paper in Austria.
Sits alone under a poplar tree.
Everyone laughs at Beethoven
because his hair explodes like his music.
His eyes spin around the sun.

Inside——he listens to all melodies,
to all planets. The Ninth Symphony
was written without a sound
from anywhere——outside.

Maybe I'll join the choir. I'll stand up
alone. My hair shooting up each syllable
until my voice spins

out of my mouth
like a comet, like a blue green fire
I have never heard sing.

hanging in space

Late evening at Lucky's Mini-mart. Sammy revs up
his flat-gray '88 Camaro. Carolyn feeling yellow
in the back seat——on crank again. Want to pull her out

but Sammy says, Get in, Sissyer,
or I'll tell your mama you smoke weed!
We take off. Screams,

Carolyn howls
with her right leg hanging out the window,
calling to guys on the street

Hey,
check this out, my man!

Sammy turns to me, talks about
his crazy uncles he lives with——

Man, they out on parole, always on my back.
His head low, chin on the steering wheel.
If it's not the teacher messin' with me
it's my *tíos*[43] loaded on *chiva*,[44] they even
make me break into houses at night with them, steal TVs
for them. It's cool, though, I got my own thing.

What about your father and mother?
No way! He says, his eyes wild. Never knew
the dude. I think he's in prison; my mother
kicked me out of the house.

Sammy stops talking. He wants
to swallow but he can't. He wants
to say more words, but he rubs the water
from his eyes
with one hand.

43. uncles
44. heroin

Couldn't handle all her rules,
her boyfriend's rules. *¡Chale!* [45]
So I moved out to my *tíos's* place
when I was in junior high.

Pulls out
another white stick.

Try some of this.
Sammy takes a hit from
the joint, jes a li'l taste,

jestaste, my man, he says.
Come on, Sissyer—have some *mota* [46]
laced with K, [47] boy.

Oooooooh, yeah.
Oooooooh, yeah. Mmmmm.

Sammy is disappearing. I blow out
and howl with Carolyn.
Rub my face, pull my lips down like a beard.

Heyyyyyyyyyyy!
Fowleeeeeeeerrrrrrvillllle!
Yooooooo Yoooooo Yooooooooooooooooo
¡Chaaaaaaaaaaleeeeeeee!

45. No way!
46. grass, marijuana
47. PCP

We swirl
through grapevine fields and railroad tracks, factory coils,
little cottage houses with amber lights, stray dogs
leaning to one side as they skip to the curbs, splattered
rows of cornstalks burned down by the sun of the Valley,
old refineries with metal jaws half open, and junkyards
with steel crushers, dark ribbed barrels and silent orange
tractors waiting, waiting, waiting
for everything to start again, in the hard work morning.

No security guards can stop us,
No vice-principal can detain us,
No teacher to make us perform,
No strangers asking us for papers
No laws to handcuff us in a sweat room
No questions, No badges, No Se Habla Españols.

On the loose, in the night, tonight
we fly, we storm, we drive, we move
we flow, we go, we live, we ride, we run
we burn, we blade, we churn, we raid
we do, we blue, we sing, we rise, we ring
we clap, we trap, we crack, we snap, we tap
we fly high, we fly low, we fly fast, we fly so high

in the blackness
in the heart of vastness
in the heart of the last heroes, *los heroes*

across the vines, across the dead orchards
across the villages of brown beetles and crickets and
dumb animals in corrals, the cows with their udders
strapped to plastic tubes and gnashing bottles,
the pigs pushing their round snouts to the demolition counter,
the chicken and turkeys squatting caged in tiny wire boxes,
we fly, across the cutting machines, the packing engines,
the hay balers, across, across, in the pesticide mist,
in the speeding phosphor haze, we fly.

Tonight, for a second,
a handful of minutes, Fowlerville
is at a standstill, we fly

cotton gins blend into the tomato-packing houses,
tan sheets of raisins stretch across thousands of acres.
I read a naked tin stamp on a fence that reads Del Monte.
I read a bright red frame on a fence that reads Sunmaid.

We rise, we fall,
we fly in this strange open heart, endless,
a dark grape jelly maze,
a depot of ancient white buses, empty, with signs
that read GROWERS CO., waiting, waiting, for the next batch
of passengers, *campesino* wives wearing scarves and
bandannas around their heads, extra-large flannel shirts,
gloves and sombreros, campesinos, this is where my father
worked, this is where my mother worked, this is
where I was born, in this blurred night of vines, we fly

we fall
we rise.
¡Aaaaaayyyyyyaaaaayyyyyaayayayayyyyyy!
¡Aaaaaaayyaayayaaayayayayayayayaayyyyyaaaaayyy!

We slide
through dirt roads, hollering, a crooked *rancho,*
a thin orchestra of desires, wires and young eyes,
the planet caves in and then it explodes, our screams
and smoke dissolve, our hot orange faces, loud cymbal hearts
clash, clash, they clash like lost warriors in the glossy blue.

We fall
we rise
¡Aaaaaayyyyyyaaaaayyyyyaayayayayyyyyy!
¡Aaaaaaayyaayayaaayayayayayayayaayyyyyaaaaayyy!

I see
my father's photograph:

Papi holds me in his arms.
Our trailer in the background—
rows upon rows of grapes in the back, further back.
Mama Lucy's photo too. She holds me up at two years,
in the sweaty light of the summer, in a labor camp
somewhere up north, maybe the Yakima Valley
When will I see my father again? I hear the crickets swing
their fuzzy pizzicato through the thick night air. Listen
to their musical ax.

I hear the pigs snort, the cows moan, the roosters screech
the beetles beep, the worms creep, the white owls swoop.

Fatherrrrrrr!
Wherrrrrre Arrrre youuuuu?
Papiiiiiiii Césaaaaarrrr?
Paaaapiiiii, Papiiiiii?
Dóndeeeeee estássssssssssssssss???
Wheeererereee areerere
yyoyououyouoouuyouuuuu?

Hey! See that ride?
Carolyn screams, bumps us, points to a rusted pickup
parked by a water pump ahead. It's mine, dude! she sings.

Mine,
looocooooooo!

Sammy and Carolyn step out,
stumble and stutter.
Break in. Carolyn
hot-wires the ignition.

Race you back to the tracks, *chavala,*
one fast mile, she says to Sammy.
Chavalaaaaaaaahhh! She screams.

Sammy barks back, he's not talking anymore
makes funny noises and sounds, he barks and
walks sideways to the car, his body out of
rhythm, his face crooked and flamey.
The K swarming.

Chavaaaaalaaaaahhh, Carolyn's scream
hangs in the air.

Are you on, Sissyer? He says to me
in crazy barks, swinging his arm like a rag.

Are yooouuuuuuuu
Ooooooooooonnnnnnnn?

Turn to Carolyn
who rolls up her window halfway, lights a smoke,
revs the truck. My body folds.

I want to run into the fields, maybe there
in the middle of the vines, in the arc
of grapes and star shaped leaves, I will
find a well, an ocean where I can jump
into its infinity, lose myself. Find myself.
I want to....

Hey, fool! Carolyn rolls down her window.
Go with Sammy, cuz I am going to smoke you guys
and he's going to need a crying partner.
Laughs with the cigarette
to one side of her mouth.

Sammy counts down, as if under water
and we fly again.

One
    Two
        Tres
            Cuatro

Black wash smears
across the windows, no sky, no moon, a weak
light from a telephone pole swishes on the windshield
for a second,

up ahead, the red lights by the railroad track are groggy.
Toward the crossing, we fly

     between plants   and steel
     between Carolyn   and us
     between Sammy   and what he sees
     between me   and tomorrow
     between what is below and what is above
     between the animals   and the worms

Sammy barks and laughs out loud, squinting
fifty to sixty to seventy miles per hour
the speed needle on the dial slides, radio blasts
a song, a country station with fuses and static
whistling, gluey voices, electronic
drums in my ears.

Carolyn's car bounces, loses control, bounces
     rollsssssssss.
          Bouncessssssssss-cessssss-cessssss.

Sammy barks again, drooling,
I am frozen

as we fly, then a boomcrash,
another BOOMCRASH, BOOM BAAAM
from the left, from the right, inside
we twist, unleashed——silent

faaaaallllllling
faaaallllllllliiiiinnnnng.

Is it up?
Are we going up?
Is it down, is it down
going down, below Great Mountain
where our animal companions live, rip the gates
little Jaguar are you there, little jag, run, run,
come, come, down we go,

in yellow watery
streaks of light and murky sparks and sizzling gasoline
rainbows over our bodies and brains

the plastic seat cushions float, in the fields
the windshield torn into chewy icicles
wrapped around a concrete light post.
Sirens from afar. Hot water comes down
my head. Sirens, water, water, down
my face.

I see
Mama Lucy.

Mama Lucy walks   away
dressed   in black.

Mama, Mama, wait! Don't leave me.
We were just going out. Friday night.

Sammy is fine, Carolyn too. I tell her
with a bird voice in my head.
Just going out. Whisper, whisper.

In the blue
and red mist
I see Mama Lucy alone. Mama——I scream
Maaammaaaaa! Maaammaaaaa!

Or is it someone, next to me
lying on the road, who screams, with his face
to one side, mouth open?

Mama Lucy presses her stomach
with her hands. See her fade
into a field of purple smoke.

See her
fade.

yellow room

Todo cambia.
Everything changes.

yellow room

Ashes
in my mouth, tastes like copper
like charcoal. I want to move my mouth
but I cannot.

My eyes are shut. Only
rings of blue light, spirals and red patches
come at me. Red fades. Where am I? Is it the sky?
Am I speaking?

A voice near me trembles—*Es mi único hijo.*
He is my only son. Mama Lucy? I recognize the voice.
Did you say that? I want to see you.

All I hear is your voice, I recognize it
by its thin sound, its kind air. The air here
smells like rubbing alcohol, the kind you
splash on yourself to stop the *vértigo*[48]—a shifting
dizzy pain, always, below your stomach, hot flashes,
sweats—*es el vértigo,* you tell me.

Then, I hold your hand,
massage your neck. Where am I, mama?
Where?

48. dizzy spells

If I stood up. If I opened my mouth and my eyes,
if I could scream—yes, a scream would do it—
if I could scream, I would wake up, my eyes clear.
I think I feel my arms.

Hairy, soft bandages with claws,
then stone, steel. Nothing.
Bandages like shells.

The arms are hanging over a spongy cushion.
My veins. Why are they running so hot? Burning.
I am on fire. A slow flame. A flame at each point
of my body. Maybe my eyes are open. Maybe
they are closed.

I can barely see. Flames go away. Go, go.
A hand, no. It's a light, tiny, shiny,
silvery, sparkles. Not a star, it could be a star.
Someone is waving it over my forehead.
A crucifix. If only

I could see my face in it. I don't feel anything.
The hand comes down to my face, my cheek.
Es mi único hijo, the kind voice says it
again, then bursts into uncontrollable tears.

How is he?
Another voice.
Wait.
Who said that?
If I could see. I recognize that voice too.
She comes closer, I tighten my neck. Curl my fingers
but I can't. Sparkles again. I can see myself reflected
on the triangles of greenish-colored glass on her jacket.

Is that my right eye? Droopy and blue-red and half closed.
Is that my mouth? Fish mouth. Swollen.
Orange and scaly. Strapped in white
tape, a tube stuck between my lips. Tubes?
Why can't I feel them?

The nose. Swollen, bloody. More tubes.
Is that me? My head is wrapped in white.
Wait a minute. Who is that breathing?
It can't be me. My chest is rising and falling
against my will. What is that machine sound?

How is he doing doctor?
I hear the triangle mirror voice again.
Is that you beside my mother, is that you Ms. Steiger?
What are you doing here? Wait. Oh, what is this tingling
inside my chest?

The sixties jacket blurs, a yellowish haze above me.
Ashes in my mouth. My tongue is somewhere
but I don't know where.

I want to scream.
My legs? My legs? I can't feel those either.
Is this how my father's leg felt?

A water bag with a tube
connects to my stomach, it's the weight
hanging to one side of my bed. I think
it is my stomach. Maybe it's my chest.

A sharp sting cuts across my face.
I jerk my head.

Easy, César. OK, easy.
A doctor. Must be. Says
she is checking the feed tube
in my nose.

Feed tube? Aghhhg! Wait,
I said something. Almost. Almost.
I heard it. I said something.

I think he is coming out of the coma.
The doctor whispers to Mama Lucy.

Twist my neck.
Tighten my jaw. Loosen it. Can't see.
Are my eyes open or closed? What is the cold plate
under my butt? Why are my legs inside cocoons?

I think I turned into a *cucaracha.*[49]
Don't laugh. Can't laugh. Can't move.

Why don't all of you just leave.
I don't need you. Don't look at me ... Wait!
My legs. Oh, my right leg. Why does it feel so heavy?

Why don't you just leave me alone.
You never knew how I was feeling, Lucy.
Yeah, I know, you pray for me and all that holy stuff
but, you left me ... alone.

I had to figure the whole thing out—
in school
in the yard
in the classroom
in the books
in the lines
in the principal's office.

49. cockroach

You never went to school
except to third grade in El Paso.
Do you hear me?

And now, you want me to wake up
just like that? Start the whole thing
over again? No way!

You can't even talk English right.
I had to learn it while everybody laughed.
Go away.

Tingling in my chest.
Is my heart beating? It is sweat? Water?
Sweat on my face, my chest. I am a giant
bubble of sweat. My body is a tear.
Or is it rain? Am I inside a rain cloud?

How are the other two?
Ms. Steiger asks the doctor.

One expired early
this morning. She says.

Expired?
Ex——pired?

The doctor said "expired"
the way Mr. Santos said "You, Mr. Garcia,
are going to Sunway Continuation."

Expired? What is expired?
Who ex-pired?

Another sharp pain bolts
through my legs. My knees
feel like giant elastic boulders full of sea water.
My stomach does not exist. It is soapy bag
with tubes hanging down by the floor. Down
where my arms dangle. Where my fingers
move
              like upside down ocean crabs.

Head traumas, severe. The doctor says.
They were racing each other, out there,
on the outskirts of town, on the road to Logan Lakes,
when one of them, the truck, lost control, rolled,
smashed against an old fire station wall. A van hit
the other one, from the left.

One dead.
The stop sign was down. She says.
Some vandals pulled the sign down.

We can't locate Sammy Luna's family.
Wasn't wearing a safety belt. Ejected from the seat.
Eighty feet from the car. In the vines.

The doctors voice rings,
echoes in my ears.

Head
trauma expired
Severe.   one expired
Early   this morning
Safety   belt ejected
Stop   sign
Taken   down in the vines
Expired   early
One   dead. One. Dead.

Sammy?
Hey, Sammy, can you hear me?
Hey *chavala,* they are saying you *expired.*
They're sellin' wolf tickets,[50] right?
Sammy? Wazup? Sammy?

50. they are "crying wolf"; lying.

Hey, hold up ...
don't listen to them, César,
forget it, it's a bad dream. Don't listen.
Come on, César, let's jam, come on
man, let's go, César,
get up ... come. Come on, loco!

Can't see.
Where are you, Sammy?
Where, man? Red red fades
into ocean blues.

No, mom!
My mother prays out loud
with her pink glass rosary.
Don't do that stuff here! In front of everybody,
come on—not in Spanish. Hey, stop it.

And what about our other student,
Carolyn Centers? Ms. Steiger asks.

She was sent home. Bruises. Face cuts.
Apparently she lives with her sister Natasha
behind their stepfather's house
in the Westside. We had a hard time
locating the guardian. The people in the other vehicle
were sent home without a scratch.

Voices fade. Mama Lucy places
the crucifix in my hand. She prays over me.
Whimpers. Sighs. Prays. Now she
is smiling. Strokes the water off my face.

He's a smart *muchacho,*
she says.

Shhh.
Don't say nothing. Mom.
Don't say . . .

Yes . . . he's been working very hard
at Sunway. He's one of my best students,
one of the wisest. Ms. Steiger says
to Mama Lucy and hugs her.

Sammy?
Carolyn?
The crumpled Camaro——behind me
a jagged heap of metal wire strips, wheels
and axles like licorice to one side, the engine
trembles, shivers——in a sheet of flames.

Hey Saaaaaammyyyyyyy … What did you say?
Where are you?

I see a blue ring,
a wavy haze, a breezy curtain
open.
It is the road. Lifting, broken. My body
in circles whirling over a bridge.
My face fading.
It is Sammy's body. Ashes. Dust. Sparks.
It is Carolyn's body. Lines, burning glass,
blood on the fence.

I am that road in flames
I am that red and yellow vapor flaring up
going into yellow-green sky, from
the front seat into the wind. Red yellows
going into to a green blue flickerdance, a leaping
leopard skin of new colors
into the dark mysterious air.

Flame——come back down.
Please, flame boy, come back.
Come back down, one more time.
Flame, can you hear me?
You ... wait ...
my mouth does not exist.
I do not exist. Do I?
My mouth is gone.
My body. Just my legs.

Who is holding my hand?
If I could only open my left eye all the way.
Papi? Hold me then. Hold me.
Papi?

No, wait. It can't be. Miguel?
Miguel Tzotzil? Nahh. Is that you?

Miguel ... I ... I ... I ... am
sorr ... Miguel ...
Can you hear me?
The feverish fingers at the end
of my hand curl around his fingers.
They tighten and let go. Miguel,
is that you? Where are you going?

I let the ocean wave flame
enter me again, burn, flicker ... leap inside
Mama holds my other hand.
I let go.
I hold on. Let go.
Falling. Rising.

Why should I ... change?
I don't change for anyone. Wait ... hold on.
Hold. Let go. I can't. I won't. Breathe.

You come back, César.
Come back, César. Her mouth opens.
Says a round word, *amor,* she says, is it a word?
The round word turns into a bigger word.
Mama Lucy screams. See her scream
through the jagged broken slivers
of light in my eyes. Can't hear her
scream. Bluish light,
spirals and emerald sparkles
flood me. Where am I?
A world of things only. Broken things.
Things and bodies. Swirl around me.
Bodies in iron scraps. The scream breaks
them, fuses them, melts them.

I am in the ocean pool in the clouds,
about to become rain, I am
inside the rain drops, floating,
falling to Great Mountain where the jaguar
calls me. I feed her with my hands of rain.
I am hiding in my mother's long hair, now
outside in the snowflakes of Denver
spinning across the sidewalk, downtown
spinning to Papi's shoulder, alone, I am in between
the tree bark waiting for the light of dawn,
I hear the sparrow sing next to me, on a branch
thin as a wire, I rise rise rise in the violet night,
in a crashing wave with all the voices of Fowlerville
inside my bones, the new crescent moon
between my chest, it is morning-star warm
I lay on top of a mountain of twisted steel,
what mountain? My school, my shredded sofa?
My pillow? A child laughs, in the fields,
with Papi planting corn. Papi carries me home
and tells me a story, then a flash, I am that story
about coming to El Norte, a Norte without
a South or East or West, a South without a Norte
forever floating, his words, Mama Lucy's words,
all words pass through me, I fall and I breathe,
for a second I dissolve into turquoise sky light.

My lips struggle, my tongue.
My legs are hot, sandy.
Hands, feet, head, swish.
Everything. Inside this new flame,
everything is a yellow-green tidal wave.
Mama Lucy's scream is that wave,
turns to gold light. Pure
lights dancing. Wait!
I can feel it, my throat,
swallow, swallow, breathe
can't swallow. I want to say.
I want to ask ...

Let the waves
carve their way back into me.
A smile fills me. Then ice, a cry.
Deep breath ... I am Lucy's scream.

¡Césssssss
            saaaaaaaaaaarr!
¡Césssssss
            saaaaaaaaaaarr!
¡Césssssssssaaaaaaaaaaaaaaaarr!

¡Amorrrrrrrrrrr!

¡Césssssaaaaaaaar!

My arms move, my feet
move too, inside the hard cocoons.
My chest swells. Voices tumble
alive. I can hear them clearly.

It will take a few months—
his legs will heal. He will have to have
that metal rod in his right leg
from now on. Crutches for while.

The doctor moves over me, fills out
a report book or something shiny
tied to my bed on a string.

César, she says—up close.
My eyes half open—César García
you—are going to make it!

César García?
Going to make it? I say
inside, to myself. Wait, doctor!
Wait! Come back!

Yellow light, rainbow spirals
above me, flow, pulse.

Hey, doctor!
I want to see Mama Lucy!
And Ms. Steiger?
And Miguel? Miguel!

I am here!
I am alive!
I want to shout
through the tape across my mouth.

Mama Lucy cleans
the water off the side of my face.
I see her
through a miniature cracked window
of tears.

Will I live? Will I survive?
Will everything be different?
Will I walk? All the voices,
the half-moon over the ocean,
my rough sparrow?

Who
will I be?

a capella

El agua es blanda, la piedra dura,
pero, gota a gota, hace cavadura.

Water is soft, rocks are hard,
but, drop by drop, water finds a way.

beginning
(at the bus stop)

At the curb of C Street, my street.
Khakis, wino shoes
blue shirt. I don't know why
I chose this shirt.

I think it reminds me of the ocean,
the repetition of the tides
like the waves that come from my heart
sometimes when I am alone.

Once Mama Lucy took me to the ocean,
I was three and she walked me to the shore.
Papi whittled wood on a bench.

I held her hand there in front of the waters, gazing
into the silvery silk moving across the horizon.

Infinity in front of me
Infinity in back of me.

It was the same all around me.
Wonder. Amazement—
I remember the ocean.

Seven weeks have come and gone.
Had to repeat orientation. Can't wait
to finish classes. Junior, next year.

I am repeating something else
here at Sunway. But,
I don't know what it is.
Sometimes I sit alone
by the snack bar. Carolyn
and Java laugh and hunch
their shoulders, excited about
things, whispering into
each other's ears. Then Carolyn sad.
Thinks about Sammy gone—

feels the scars across the side of her face,
feels the night come across her eyes, a rapid
shadow, icy and deep. Thinks about Sammy gone.
Touches up her dark makeup, giggles, turns to me
for a second, remembers:

Sammy sits in the back row, Mrs. Tinko's.
She calls on Mariah Martínez to discuss the idea of balance,
what is tone? Romeo and Juliet. Sammy, in the back,
breaks off the flat screws from our table. Bangs the legs
on the floor. Mrs. Tinko listens to Mariah carefully
pronounce the words—*balance, tone.* Bang again.

Big bang.
Little bang.
Big bang. Sammy plays
his piano, he is Beethoven in black baggies,
his torch of gelled hair, up and wild. Listen
to Sammy play his concerto, his one hard boy
symphony. Sammy cackles, laughs out—

Hey teacher,
hey, here's my *tone!*

Good, good, Mariah.
Very good, Mariah.
Dogs Sammy.

I look at Carolyn and Java, think
maybe they could be my sisters
maybe they are my sisters.

Java's a black girl who got
kicked out of Lincoln High
for low grades.

Java is honest,
she says things are different now,
she smiles and I know she is smiling
for real——the way sunlight covers everything
not just one special place
like a rose patch or the young grass
reeds when they first come out
of the earth. Java smiles.

Little John came up to me
yesterday, said

So, wazup, Sissyer
    are you weak,
are you going to talk,
flap your mouth
in front of an audience
or are you going show me
if you're down?

My name is César——
César García. OK? Start with that.

Are you approaching me?
I asked him.

If you are
then, let's handle it.
Wait a minute? Why don't
we take it all the way to Sammy?

Little John cocks his head
to one side. Didn't expect
me talking tough. Backs down.
Says
        You're *loco*, man.

What am I repeating?

The fights?
The language?
The time I spend alone?
The walls that contract and expand?
The teachers searching for answers in my eyes?
The little mother at home who prays for me?
The fender inside my chest with pointed chrome claws.
This stone that turns to water?

What am I repeating?

My head bows. Remember Sammy gone.
Remember Papi gone. All gone.
A rough sigh passes across my chest,
a light-footed jaguar with shiny eyes, eager eyes,
a rumbling sigh that purrs.

Step in.
Breathe, breathe, César. I say to myself.
Take your time.
Take your time.

I can hear Sammy cracking up—
Hey, Sissyer, where's your *chavala* crutches?
Then nothing comes back.

Tough wheels
roll, churn across the pavement.
Bus tumbles through space and carries us to school.
Faces, lights, leaves, wires, busted cars and fences wash by,
they flash and smear across the window.

I am changing.
I breathe a little deeper. My mouth opens
as if to say I am here today, as if to begin
to say things.

I am walking again, without crutches.
Drag one foot, like my father.
I am beginning.

birds fly in
a bird shape

Outside our tiny apartment, C Street. Saturday.
On the stairs. Traffic. A siren sprays
red light into the haze.

I notice the sky a wash of clouds,
an old woman that could be Dolores,
my grandmother, who lives in El Paso, Texas.

Breathe in and pull at the feathery grass
breaking through the sidewalk. Cartoon
voices stumble out through the screen door.

I am sitting still. No more crutches.
Move my right foot a little. Follow
a serious ant carrying a dead bug back home.

The sky looks bigger today.
At the edges, the blue

becomes whitish and fades into the light
over the orange mountains.

Above me,
at my zenith, the sky pours into a pool

of deep turquoise. A sky vase, flowery and infinite.
There is a family of birds crossing over telephone wires.
Notice how they swim next to each other.

They form another bird. The wings, the tender
neck and face, the little spaces in between
form the bird. Connected to each other,

one bird.
Many birds,

one bird. Birds fly in bird shapes, yes.
I notice people strolling across the street. Some
walk into Bradley's Burgers, others wait for a bus.

What shape do we walk in, all of us,
in one moment? Carlos Johnson, Carolyn,
Maxy? Miguel?

A bird shape, a gun, a violin? I sit. Stretch
my legs. Wrinkle my nose, sing a little song.

sentence structure

The bell rings fast. Ms. Steiger says
take out your books. Turn to Sentence Structure—
exercise on *ambiguity*.

Ambiguity? Asks Carolyn, shakes her new purple hair.
Smiles, stretches her lips wide to her kinky double earrings.

Ms. Steiger mentions the holocaust,
she mentions the six million Jews
taken down
to Nazi gas chamber showers, to the dental tortures
to human skin lamps, to mass graves alive,
in Auschwitz, in Bergen Belsen,
she mentions the abyss where violence blossoms.

Write your response, Ms. Steiger says.
I write fast.

Write long notes
in my journal.
I write complete sentences
without ambiguity. I write about death,
about losing someone I know, about the little white cross
Mama Lucy, me and Carolyn put up for Sammy,
his road-cross with red yellow plastic flowers
at the stop light on the way to Logan Lakes, I write
about going down in the night, through ripping steel
and blood flying and waking up with busy machines
pumping through my chest, about being buried
alive in a coma, I write about coming back,
steel rods in my right leg, I write about
absence, about my father who never calls,
my father who has left me.

Who are your heroes?
Ms. Steiger asks.

Killers can be heroes.
Peacemakers can be heroes.
  Ms. Steiger says in a low voice and
  paces across our small smooth tables.

Who are your heroes?
Ms. Steiger asks once more, as if
singing a sad and hopeful song.

I write about the man in the poster
on the wall, by the computers—César Chávez,
about campesinos, about how they work the land,
about their families, like my family, always on the run,
Mexicanos who speak Spanish to the tiny plants, Filipinos
and Hmong, the poor. I write about their hardships—
separations, pesticides, *la migra.*[51] I write
about Mama Lucy. She is my hero.

Mama Lucy has been taking English
classes at night. Works hard.
Brings books home, we read them together.
She even reorganized the *Workshop Tips*
magazines my father left.

51. Immigration Patrol

51. Immigration Patrol

143

Mama Lucy says we must go back
to Rambling West High.

Hay que saber hablar.
You have to speak up.

Nunca es tarde.
It is never too late.

After school, she tells me.
I have arranged a meeting.

We meet with my old principal,
Dr. Bongosto in his carpeted office—
flowers and yearbooks, trophies
and post cards.

Mama Lucy
is speaking up.

Mr. Stanton, school policeman
is here too. Next to mama, Mr. Santos
rubs his hands on his knees.

My son, César, was hurt here.
He is still hurt. Look at him.
Mama says. Why you pull him
out of recess last semester?

Why Mr. Stanton search him?
Why don't you call me?
Why so many Saturday schools
doing *nada* while teacher reads the paper?

Mr. Santos's face reddens
into a radish with a skinny tie.

I did what I am supposed to do, he says.
Looks at his report on his lap.
Sits very still—Cesar was with a group of boys
that were squaring off against the Hmongs.

A fight was next. Right?
A fight! Who knows what could've happened.
Mr. Santos adjusts his tan sport coat.

You no right to search him and detain him
without any reason. You could have call me.
César was new to Rambling West. She says this,
sitting on a thick brown leather chair, her feet barely
touching the carpet. She says this
with her eyes on his eyes.

I have never seen Lucy speak up.
This is the principal's office. My head feels stiff.

Lucy and I
have never been here together.

Mr. Santos rolls his eyes. Dr. Bongosto pulls
at his nostrils with his thumb and finger.
Mrs. Garcia, we're glad you came ... uh ... and
we'll see what ... uh ... we can do.

You do something ... now!
Mama Lucy leans forward
and stares at Mr. Bongosto.

Mr. Stanton clears his throat
and rushes his words: Dr. Bongosto,
you know what happened
to Lincoln High; they were searching students
without cause. Remember?

Mama interrupts. César will be back
next semester. What about other students here like César?
You know what happened
to Sammy Luna. Don't you?

Both straighten their ties
at the same time. Nod, look at each other.

He didn't have to die that way.
She says, turns to one side of her chair,
her eyes on Mr. Santos's eyes.

Sammy Luna didn't' have to die
that way. He didn't have to die
so young.

Mama Lucy gets a wild idea.
Why don't I do Saturday schools? New kind.
Where kids just don't show up because
they ditch class during week.

I'll tell stories,
Teach *enchiladas,*
sing *corridos.*

Una canción crea una tradición.
One song starts a tradition. She says,
almost singing in Spanish! With her arms
up, out of the chair, almost dancing
in the tiny auditorium of steely faces.

Mr. Santos's eyebrows go back crazy.
My head bobs up.

I am going to talk to Ms. Steiger
at Sunway too, maybe sessions after school. Monday
and Wednesdays? She says with music in her voice,
standing, then moving through the office.

Lucy's been calling
other parents at Sunway.
I know she's doing it for me.

Never seen my Mama Lucy like this.
Speaking up. For me. With me.
In Mr. Bongosto's office!

Well, I am not sure … the superintendent …
you understand, this is highly out of line …

Melendez and Estrada need something
like this. Mr. Stanton butts in. I just busted them
yesterday for wearing colors.

You mean burgundy?
The school colors?
Mama Lucy interrupts.
No, ma'am. You know anything
close to red is a gang color.

Why not *los football boys,*
they wear the same colors in the halls.
She sits down slow and stretches
her right eye wide open
with her finger. I see them
with my eyeballs!

But, ma'am
that's different ... and ... uh ...
Avoids
Mama Lucy's fiery wild eye.

Mr. Bongosto orders Mr. Santos
to arrange Mama Lucy's visit
for one Saturday only. To start,
well, to ... he says, as he fumbles
for the proper sentence.

a capella

Maxy Ortega, in the second row
thinks about football. He can see the touchdown
just a few inches from his feet. Java
on the far right corner thinks about her baby
Carlton, three months old, back home
with her mother.

In the back,
about six seats behind me, Monreal, the new guy
thinks about yesterday when he got home.
He pulled out a snack-bar meat loaf
from his pocket. Asked his mother,

¿Qúe es esto?
What is this?

Monreal
had never seen meat loaf.
He's here because he talked back in Spanish
to his science teacher.

Kat and Carolyn are mad
because they are getting dogged
by Shane Morrison. No more CR[52]
for me says Carolyn to Kat.
Kat fixes her giant hair. Chews gum
with her glossy orange lips
half open.

Little John, the baritone,
sits next to me, to my left.
He's thinking he's in trouble. Talked
to Sammy's girl, Marlene,
at the lockers.

Nobody
flirts with Sammy's girl. Even
if he is gone. Sammy's guys
will wait for him, after school.

52. crank

Carlos Johnson peers into the sky
through the windows. A blue thin fan
with fast shadows and quiet trees.
He is thinking about yesterday's assignment.

Ms. Steiger said, Write about who you are.
Carlos Johnson laughed. Is something funny?
She asked. How can I write about myself?
I don't even know what I am.

I don't know if I am black.
I don't know if I am Mexican.
My parents never talk about it.
That's it, Carlos. Write that.
Ms. Steiger smiled a big smile.
It was the first time
I heard Carlos
talk in class. It was the first time
I heard he was Mexican *and* black.

Gold flashes
through the leaves outside the window. I turn my face.
Think about the year since I started at Rambling West.
Sunway. Think about next year.
Graduation. My father.

Think about Miguel who left to Mexico
without saying a word.

After school practice choir.
African American Spirituals.
Extra credit, says Ms. Steiger.

You have a beautiful voice. You are singing a solo
for our last school assembly this year.
We warm up in Spanish:

AHHHH
EHHHH
EEEEEE
OOOO
UUUUU
EHHHHL
BUUU
RROOO
SAAAA
BEEEE
MAAAS
QUEEEH
TUUU

AEIOU—
¡El burro sabe más que tú!
The mule knows more than you!
Mama Lucy says as we rehearse.
She comes to class on Wednesdays
to teach us proverbs.

We are wearing jade-green robes on stage.
Front row: Carolyn, Java, Lucretia and Maijue,
a new girl from Rambling West
sing soprano and alto, sing high Gs
Second row:
Tenors—me and Carlos Johnson and Cheyenne,
a runaway boy from West Liberty, Iowa.

Tenors—sounds like
tenedores in Spanish—*forks.*
Some of the guys call us dorks.
Fork dorks. It doesn't matter.

Third and fourth rows: Baritones and basses
Little John who flicks my ear, Maxy Ortega
who flicks Little John's stubby head and

Monreal and Barlow who sing
with their mouth almost shut.

Ms. Steiger sings as she directs us, a capella
without music,

just your voices, without music
she says. You must make your own music
with your own voices, together,
in harmony, in the melody——
A capella.

Raises her hands, her palms open
like letting rain dance on her fingertips,
turns to me,
bows ...

If you get there before I do
tell all of my friends I am comin' too.

My voice flies out of my mouth
I don't know if it is a bird or a cat or a jaguar.
I can see Mama Lucy sitting in the front row.
She brings her hands up to her face.

I looked over yonder and what did I see?
Comin' for to carry me home ...

Voices rush behind me,
voices rush in front of me:

swing low, sweet chariot,
comin' for to carry me home ...

I hear Maxy hit a low E!
I hear Carolyn hit the impossible high G!

See the eyes sparkle in the audience.
They shimmer together in one sea. A sea of birds
that flutter like water, like light.

Every note carries my memories.
My mouth is open three fingers wide, like
Ms. Steiger says. Open to sing.

My chest is open too.
I am standing tall with my voice growing
out of me, a flame, a spark, a corn plant in green gold.
Every note carries the roads to Fowlerville,
the twists and turns, the fights and screams,
the nights alone and the days lost in sad dreams.
I am singing out.